Angry Waters

ALSO BY WALT MOREY

Gentle Ben
Home Is the North
KÄVIK the Wolf Dog

Walt Morey

Angry Waters

ILLUSTRATED BY RICHARD CUFFARI

17246

E. P. DUTTON & CO., INC.

NEW YORK

For Lee Anna Deadrick
whose help has been invaluable

Author's Note

Persons who know the Columbia River region will realize that I have "adjusted" the geography of the country to accommodate the plot. The locations of islands, dikes, and fictional towns along the river obviously do not coincide with fact.

—W.M.

Illustrations

one

Mr. Edwards picked up Dan at the courthouse in Portland and they started driving up the valley in the rain. Through the streaming windshield Dan watched as the city's buildings thinned out and fell behind.

Open country began to appear. The farms were clusters of old paint-peeling buildings. Rusting machinery sat about some of them. At intervals they passed farm animals. They all seemed to be standing with an air of miserable dejection, heads down, backs humped against the rain. Pools dotted the land and water snaked in coffee-brown rivulets across rough-plowed fields. For the first time Dan Malloy began to realize what he had let himself in for, and gloom settled over him.

Mr. Edwards kept glancing at him, measuring him with a black-browed frown. Finally he said in a flat voice, "You're smaller than I expected."

"I'm tall enough," Dan said.

"There's more to bigness than height."

"How big do you think I should be?" Dan didn't like the man's matter-of-fact voice or his words.

"Big enough to pitch hay, pack a sack of grain, maybe wrestle a calf," Mr. Edwards answered promptly.

"You want a Sampson." Belligerence crept into Dan's voice. "You don't want me. That's fine. I don't want any part of a farm. You can turn around and take me back."

Mr. Edwards drove in scowling silence for a minute. Then he wheeled to the side of the highway, stopped the car and shut off the motor. He twisted in the seat and looked at Dan with somber gray eyes. Frank Edwards was tall, lean muscled, with a bony, wind-tanned face and a square jaw. His shoulders were heavy, his chest wide. He looked as if he'd done a lot of hard work. He said to Dan in an even voice, "I guess you and I had better have an understanding."

"About what?"

"Not about that gang you ran around with, or holding up the supermarket."

"I didn't do any of that holdup," Dan said. "I drove the car. I didn't even know the car was stolen and I didn't know they planned a stickup. Rocky had me drive because I'm the best driver. When he said to stop and wait for them I did."

"I know all that. You were pretty stupid," Mr. Edwards said. "Maybe that's one reason the judge put you on parole instead of sending you to Hill View with the rest, or to that Halfway House, which is next to the big pen. That's where your head man, that Rocky Nelson, went."

"You know it all," Dan said. "What's there to talk about?"

"Plenty. I was led to believe that I was coming down here to get a boy that'd been running around with the wrong gang and had just accidentally got into trouble. That he'd be glad to go to a good home on a year's probation. And I thought that's how it was when I listened to the judge talking to you this morning. Now you sound pretty tough and belligerent and I'm not sure. I've got to be sure, boy. I want to know more about you before I take you into my home. Maybe I *will* turn around right here and take you back."

"You heard everything this morning," Dan said.

"Seems like I missed some, so tell me again. You've been living with an uncle the past five years. Where's your folks?"

"Dead. Uncle Harry was Dad's brother."

"What's he do?"

Dan shrugged. "He's got some kind of pension."

"He wasn't there this morning. Why not?"

"He's out someplace with friends. He's been gone a couple of days."

"He leaves you alone a lot, eh?"

"I make out all right."

"Sure. That's why you were in court. You're in second-year high school but you don't attend regularly. They say you spent most of your time hanging out with that gang. Why'd you join a gang?"

"Why not?" The man's digging was arousing Dan's anger. "I guess you don't know much about city kids." He'd been left alone a lot, especially the last couple of years. Uncle Harry was always gone when he had money. He returned only when he was broke, and then he was usually sick. The juvenile authorities had been out to the house a number of times, but luckily Uncle Harry had been home each time and fairly sober, so nothing had come of their visits. He'd joined the gang because it gave him a place to go, friends to be with. When Rocky had first asked him to join he had lied about his age, telling them he was sixteen, for fear they'd reject him if he said he was fifteen. At fifteen he was the youngest by almost two years. Rocky was about nineteen. Dan knew the gang accepted him because he was good with cars and motors. They'd had him working on their old cars a lot. Rocky most of all. But Dan didn't mind. The gang was a sort of family for him. With them there was the feeling of belonging, of being needed. He was part of something.

But this big, stolid man who kept needling him with questions would never understand that. So he just looked out the window at the rain-pooled world and waited for the next question.

Mr. Edwards turned away from questions about the gang and asked, "This morning when the judge asked if you were agreeable to going to a farm you said 'yes.' Now you're not. What kind of an act was that?"

"No act. I didn't have any choice." But that wasn't the reason. Right after their arrest the whole gang had been held in a detention room for an hour, and Rocky had advised him. "Play it smart. Don't give 'em any trouble. Go along with everything they say. It'll be easier for you. I know." And Rocky did know. He'd been through this twice before.

So Dan had gone along. But driving out into the country now and passing these soaked, dreary-looking farms with their muddy fields running water and old paint-chipped buildings had changed his mind. Rocky or no Rocky, he wanted no part of living on one of these farms. "You can get rid of me easy," Dan said. "Just turn around and take me back and tell them you've changed your mind. It'll make us both happy."

Mr. Edwards studied the boy beside him for a long moment. He saw a rather tall, but very thin boy with straight sandy hair and a sprinkling of freckles across a short nose. There was a stubborn set to his jaw and his blue eyes were steady and defiant. Frank Edwards scrubbed a hand across his face and dug fingers through his hair. He said, "Hm-m-m, hm-m-m," and shook his head as if he'd made up his mind but didn't like the decision.

Finally he said in the bluntest possible voice, "I didn't like this idea from the beginning. I got talked into it. Now that I see you I like it even less. I can use an extra hand on the farm but I don't figure you're it. You're not satisfied either. It seems we both made a bum deal." Mr. Edwards rubbed his jaw hard. "But I'm no quitter. If I start a thing I never drop it until I've given it the big try. I'm going to do that with you, even though my better judgment says it's no use. So I guess you and I will have to make the best of being stuck with each other, boy." With that Mr. Edwards started the car and pulled back onto the highway. Dan, huddling in the corner of the seat and looking out at the

13

rain-drenched land, felt angry and trapped. They traveled for several hours and Mr. Edwards spoke only once, to ask Dan if he was hungry. Dan said, "No," though he was. It was the only act of defiance he had left.

The road shrank from four lanes to two. The two became a narrow ribbon that followed the river. The towns grew smaller, the farm homes fewer as the empty miles fell behind. It was late afternoon when they finally turned off the road, ran up a lane, and stopped at an old house perched on a barren knoll.

"This's it." Mr. Edwards unfolded his long length from behind the wheel.

Dan got out stiffly dragging his old suitcase. At that moment a dog rounded the corner of the house. He was a huge black beast with long hair streaming water. He had a big head tapering down to powerful jaws. His mouth was open in a wicked grin showing rows of tearing teeth. He looked at Dan, head lowered in the most menacing gesture Dan had ever seen. Then he made for the boy, barking at the top of his lungs and every tooth in his head bared.

Dan stumbled back. He struck the side of the car. The next instant he was trapped there as the dog reared up against him, front paws slamming into his chest. Those gleaming teeth were only inches from Dan's throat. And the dog's hot breath fanned his face. He started to yell in fright. Then Mr. Edwards yanked the dog down. "Beat it, Nipper," he said.

The dog trotted away through the rain looking back at Dan over his shoulder.

Mr. Edwards swung a long arm. It took in the old house, the buildings below, a great expanse of rain-pooled field crisscrossed by fences. At the far end of the field ran the gray streak of the river, and beyond that rose the solid bulk of the hills. "The farm," he said, and Dan caught the note of pride in his voice. "One hundred and eighty acres of some of the finest dairy land in the state."

Just as bad as the farms they'd been passing, Dan thought, and a great loneliness went crying through him. Without a word he followed Mr. Edwards into the house.

There were two women in the warm kitchen and Mr. Edwards said, "Doris, Jennie, this is Dan Malloy."

Doris Edwards was a trim, neat woman with a ready smile and a single small streak of gray through her soft brown hair. Dan thought, About forty, maybe a little more. Then she smiled and he was sure forty was too much. "Dan," she said, "we're glad to have you." Her voice was warm and friendly.

Jennie, the girl, was about fourteen and slender. She had shining long blonde hair and her mother's quick smile. She said, "Hi, Danny."

Her brown eyes were so direct that Dan just clutched his old suitcase and looked away embarrassed.

Mr. Edwards said abruptly, "Guess I'd better get moving. It's time to do chores." He turned abruptly out of the house.

Doris Edwards said, "Dan, put your suitcase here in the corner. Jennie, why don't you take Dan out and show him around? You can gather the eggs and bring them in."

"Okay," Jennie said, "be ready in a minute." She disappeared through a door. Dan waited and looked about the kitchen. The house had tremendously high ceilings and the old-fashioned heavy woodwork that he'd seen in several houses in the older section of the city. But unlike those others this house looked well kept up. The wallpaper was clean and not torn anywhere; the woodwork had been freshly painted. The kitchen furniture was old but sturdy. A big square table, already set for dinner, occupied one corner of the kitchen. Above the table were glassed-in cupboards filled with neat stacks of dishes. Everything else in the kitchen was modern. An electric stove in one corner, a toaster, electric coffeepot on the table. These things surprised him. He didn't know exactly what he'd expected, a wood stove probably.

Jennie reappeared dressed in boots and a yellow slicker. Dan followed her outside and down the mud-slick hill toward the barn. "You should have heavy shoes and a raincoat for out here," she said.

"They're in my suitcase." It seemed he should say more to her, but the only thing he could think of was, "You always lived out here?"

"Five years," Jennie smiled. "Dad was a construction man. But he was raised on a farm. He couldn't wait to get back to one."

The barn was a huge cavernous building that smelled of hay, grain, and another scent that he was to learn was cows. Jennie stopped at a small window and said, "We can watch from here. Dad's going to let them in."

About twenty cows stood in the ankle-deep mud of the barn lot, heads bent against the drive of the rain. Mr. Edwards, in overalls and boots, opened the back door and yelled, "All right, bring 'em in, Nipper."

The black dog shot out the door and circled the cows, barking and making threatening dashes at the laggards. In a moment he had them milling toward the door. He turned to dash back and nip the heels of a slowpoke to send her bawling and hightailing after the rest.

The cows streamed into the barn, jostling and shoving, swinging their heads, wicked horns gleaming. Each cow made for a special stanchion, thrust her head through, and began eating the grain in the box.

The barn was a noisy place with twenty cows popping their hoofs and rattling their iron stanchions. A motor banged away in a far corner. Rain hammered steadily on the sheet-iron roof, filling the huge interior with a hollow roar. Nipper trotted importantly back and forth behind the cows.

Dan watched as Mr. Edwards washed off the cow's udders, then got the milking machine hooked up to the two nearest cows. Dan was amazed. He had thought they'd be milked by hand.

Nipper came and sat on his tail beside Dan. He ran out his tongue, showed his long teeth, and looked up at the boy with tawny eyes. Dan moved away.

Jennie said, "Come on," and led Dan down an aisle which came out at the head of the feeding cattle. "I like to watch them eat," she said.

Dan looked down the row of munching heads. Each cow's name was printed on its stanchion. There were Bell, Bonnie, Ginger, Snowflake, Fawn, Rusty, and some fourteen or fifteen more. "I guess you get a lot of milk," he observed.

"About eighty gallons."

"A day?" Dan asked amazed. "What do you do with so much?"

"Sell it to the co-op."

"What's that?"

"A lot of farmers joined together to sell their milk. They make cheese, butter, ice cream, and bottle some milk for stores. Dad's president and Mom's secretary. Gee, you don't know much," Jennie said.

"I've never been on a farm." Dan reached out to touch the nearest cow. She tossed up her head, her horn struck his arm with numbing force.

"That's Ginger," Jennie said. "She's sort of skittish. But she'll get used to you. She's dry now."

"Dry?" Dan asked.

"She doesn't give milk now," Jennie explained as they walked down the line of cows. "She's going to have a calf soon, then she'll give milk again. Dairy cows have to have a calf every year to keep up their milk production." She stopped before another cow and patted her head. "This is Blossom. You can pet her or do anything. She's a baby. She's going to have a calf, too. She'll go dry in a few weeks."

Dan stretched a hand and gingerly patted the cow between the eyes. She looked up at him, her eyes big and soft. Then she stretched her head across the manger and licked his pants. Dan patted her again.

They walked to the end of the line of cows and Jennie said, "This is Junior."

Junior was in a box stall made of sturdy planks. He was the fiercest-looking animal Dan had ever seen. A chain was looped tight about his horns and fastened to a timber. There was a ring in his nose and another chain was fastened to a ring that was secured to the stanchion. Junior snorted and pawed and glared at Dan with red-rimmed eyes. He shook his head, rattling his chains. Suddenly he lunged across the stanchion at Dan. He was brought up short by the chain around his horns. He continued to snort and paw and glare. A bellow rumbled deep in his chest. A wave of fear washed over Dan and he jumped back.

"He's mean as sin," Jennie said. "But he's an awfully good bull. Just don't get close enough so he can butt you."

Mr. Edwards called, "Jennie, you gathered the eggs yet?"

"Would you like to come with me and see the brooder house where the baby chicks are, and the laying house, Danny?"

"It's Dan," he said stiffly. "Not Danny."

"I'm sorry," she murmured.

As they went out the barn door she explained, "Gathering the eggs and checking the baby chicks is my job every night."

The brooder house was about ten feet square. It was warm inside. A flat, round, electrically heated sheet-metal form with canvas sides was suspended about six inches above the floor. Jennie raised a trap door in the brooder and Dan saw several hundred fuzzy yellow chicks milling about underneath. "As long as they don't bunch up," Jennie explained, "they're all right. When they begin crowding together they're cold. Then I turn up the rheostat and give them more heat until they spread out again."

"What happens if you don't?"

"They trample each other to death. Half of them could

be dead by morning. But they're fine now. Let's go to the laying house."

The laying house was a long, narrow building, lit by three bare bulbs. Like the other buildings, it was old. At least two hundred white chickens scratched and sang industriously in the six-inch-deep straw. One end of the house was lined with rows of nests. Jennie began gathering eggs from the bottom row and putting them in a huge wire basket. "You can take the top row, Danny. It's a little high for me to reach."

"Not Danny . . ." he began, annoyed.

"I forgot," she said quickly. "But you look like a Danny."

"What's that mean?"

Her brown eyes were big and solemn and their direct look annoyed him.

"I don't know," she said. "You just do."

Dan began gathering eggs to get away from her eyes. In the fourth nest he found a hen. He could see the ends of eggs peeping from under her. He slid his hand in carefully and got one. Her head shot out and she pecked his wrist. He dropped the egg in surprise and it broke. A half dozen hens were there instantly and had eaten it in seconds.

"Darn her!" Jennie reached in purposefully and tossed the hen out. "She's always trying to sleep in the nests."

She filled the basket. Dan had never seen so many eggs at one time. "How many have we got?" he asked.

"More than a hundred."

"They laid all these today?"

"Of course," Jennie said. "You can carry the basket to

the house. Just be careful you don't slip and fall." She smiled, "A hundred eggs can make an awful mess."

Supper was of such a variety and quantity as Dan had never known. He was so lonesome he had thought he wouldn't be able to eat. But he looked at his plate piled high with roast beef, creamed peas, potatoes and rich brown gravy. The aroma of the food-laden table assailed his nostrils. The juices began to flow in his mouth and he found himself eating. It was the kind of meal and homelike atmosphere he'd never had with his uncle. They talked about their particular interests and activities, each offering comments. There was nothing Dan could take part in so he ate in silence and listened.

Jennie was annoyed with the boy across the aisle in her study hall. "He spends almost the whole period looking around to see who's watching him and combing his hair. Every time I look up he's combing his hair and making with the teeth."

"Doing what?" Doris Edwards asked.

"Grinning, Mom. He's always grinning at me."

"Sounds like you're watching him pretty close," Mr. Edwards said in a dry voice.

"I am not," Jennie insisted indignantly. "But I have to look up sometimes."

"And it's easier to look at Eddie making with the—the teeth," Mrs. Edwards smiled.

"Well," Jennie defended, "if I don't look in his direction then I have to look behind me or out the window, and then Miss Ryan wants to know why I'm doing that."

"You've got a tough problem," Doris Edwards agreed

seriously. "The only solution I see is to keep your nose and eyes buried in your books. You might bring up your grades a little if you did, especially in math."

"Oh, Mom," Jennie grumbled and subsided into silence.

Mr. Edwards said, "The storm didn't seem so bad in the city. I guess all the buildings cut down the wind. But parking seems to be getting worse every time I go in. I'd sure hate to buck that traffic every day. Give me the country every time."

"I used to like the city," Doris Edwards said. "Big stores, crowds of people rushing about, the feeling of exciting things happening."

"You'd like to go back?" Mr. Edwards asked.

"I said 'used to,'" Doris Edwards smiled. "I'm a country gal now and I wouldn't trade it for all the cities in the world."

So the meal went, the conversation light and cheerful and personal. But none of it touched Dan. He kept his eyes on his plate and finished his dinner, feeling excluded and alone.

Afterward Mr. Edwards went into the big living room, settled himself in an easy chair, and began to read the paper. Jennie and her mother started clearing the table. Doris Edwards said, "Make yourself at home, Dan. There's a lot of hunting and fishing magazines in the rack in the living room."

Dan picked up the first magazine he came to, sat down, and idly began flipping the pages. But he wasn't interested. He could hear the wind slamming against the corners of the house. Rain drove against the dark window near him and big drops slid down the glass in ragged wind-blown trails. Across the room Mr. Edwards was buried in the paper, just the top of his dark head showing. At intervals the paper rustled as he turned the pages. From the kitchen came the clatter of dishes and the sounds of the two women's voices.

Finally the noises in the kitchen ceased. Jennie came into the living room with her books and settled under the hanging light at the big round oak table. As she studied she frowned and bit on her pencil. She glanced up at last and asked, "What year were you in high, Danny?"

"Second," he said.

"You going to start school here?"

"I don't know."

Mr. Edwards' eyes came to him over the top of the paper, but he said nothing. After a moment he returned to his reading.

"This's my first year," Jenny said. "I sure hate this old math. I hope you start school here." She bent over the book again.

Doris Edwards came to the door and said, "Dan, would you like to see your room? I took your suitcase up."

Jennie smiled and said, "Good night, Danny."

Dan said, "Good night."

Mr. Edwards glanced up briefly, then he shook out his paper and returned to reading.

Dan followed Doris Edwards up a narrow stairs where she pushed open the door to a room and said, "Yours. It's the only room up here. I fixed it as best I could with the furniture we had. You feel free to move things about any way you like."

Dan walked into the room and started to look around.

Doris Edwards said, "I know how you're feeling, Dan, and it's perfectly natural. I felt the same way the first time I left home. But it's going to be all right."

Dan turned and said bluntly, "No, it won't. With you and Jennie maybe my staying here would be all right. But not with Mr. Edwards."

"Why do you say that?" Doris Edwards sat down on the edge of the bed and gripped the blanket on either side of her. Her eyes were big and brown and as direct as Jennie's.

"He was pretty disappointed when he saw me. He needs somebody bigger and stronger."

"You two have had a talk?"

"On the way home."

"I see." She considered Dan a moment. "You are a little thin. But give me a few weeks and I'll put another ten pounds on you. And with the outdoor exercise and fresh air you'll soon have muscles like a Hercules," she smiled.

"That's not enough," Dan said. "He needs somebody that knows about farming, about bulls and cows and chickens and things. I know about cars and motors."

"A smart boy like you will learn in no time."

Dan shook his head. "Even if I got the muscle and the know-how it still wouldn't work. We just don't hit it off. He told me he never liked the idea of taking a boy."

"That's true," Doris Edwards agreed. "The whole thing was my idea. We always wanted a boy as well as a girl, especially Frank did. Then last summer when we could have used an extra man during the heavy haying I began thinking of taking a boy. A friend who works with boys helped me talk Frank into it. Frank's slow and cautious,

Dan. We have to give him a little more time to adjust to this. He will, believe me. He's fair and he's honest."

Dan shook his head. "I'm a city kid. I don't belong on a farm."

"Which means you don't like what you've seen so far," Doris Edwards said. "I didn't either at first. I was a city girl. My father was a construction man. That's how I met Frank. When we first moved out here I hated the isolation, being miles from the nearest neighbor or a town. I didn't like the strange animals, the rain and mud. Now I know that what I thought was isolation is really peace and quiet. I learned that every animal has a different personality, just like people. And that the rain and mud of winter makes the grass rich and green in spring. Then I began to like it here."

"You think I'll like it?"

"Perhaps. If you become interested, if you let yourself become involved in the activities here. It's hard to hate things you understand and are interested in. All I'm really trying to say is, give yourself a little time to know us and to know this place. Give us time to know you. We've all got to make a few adjustments. Don't jump to a conclusion and decide to hate a thing until you know what it is you're hating." She rose, smiling, "My, I didn't think I'd say so much." She started to leave, then added soberly, "I want this to work, Dan. I want it very much for all of us."

Dan listened to her go down the stairs. Then he closed the door. The room was small, and right up under the roof. He could hear the endless beat of the rain and the dismal moaning of wind at the corners of the house. There was a bed, a dresser and mirror, and a closet for the few clothes he'd brought. A double window overlooked the yard. He went to the window and looked out. A black mantle hid the valley and he barely made out the outline of the barn and laying house. In the city there were always corner streetlights and porch lights to chase the deepest dark. He thought about that, his mind a hundred miles away. A door slammed and directly below him Dan made out Mr. Edwards' tall shape going down the hill toward the barn carrying a flashlight.

"You're alone here," he told himself, "with three complete strangers, a brute of a bull that wants to break every bone in your body, a big black dog that's waiting to sink his teeth in your throat, and twenty cows. And you're stuck here for a whole year."

He thought briefly of running away. But that was no good. They'd just catch him and bring him back. There was only one thing he could do, continue to follow Rocky's advice. Go along with this farm thing, make it as easy on himself as possible.

All right. He could keep away from Junior, the bull. He was always tied. The cows would mostly be in their stanchions when he was around, or out in the fenced-in pasture. No problem there. He'd learn what he could and try to get along with Mr. Edwards. But that big black ugly dog. That Nipper. He could still feel the dog's weight slamming into his chest and see those teeth within an inch of his throat. He had a real fear of the dog. The only thing he could do was ignore Nipper and keep as far away from him as possible. And never forget to keep one eye on him. If he could do all these things maybe he'd get through the year all right.

two

When Dan awoke it was still raining. The window was black-dark and it was deathly still throughout the house. He listened to the rain hammer on the roof and thought about this place, these people, and the animals. He was thinking how he was stuck here for a whole year when he heard a step on the stairs. He lay perfectly still while the slow, measured tread climbed toward his room. It had to be Mr. Edwards, but why would he be coming up here in the middle of the night? A rush of fear froze him to the bed.

The door creaked open and Dan made out the lean bulk of Mr. Edwards against the inner dark. He stood there looking in and Dan could feel the man's eyes probing toward him. He lay still as long as he could, then he knew he would have to move or explode.

Mr. Edwards' voice said softly into the silence, "You awake?"

"Yes," Dan managed.

"You want to come down and help with the milking?"

Dan sat up, "What time is it?"

"Five thirty."

"Five thirty!"

"That's how it is on a farm," Mr. Edwards said. "I'll go ahead and get started."

Dan crawled out of bed, got his heavy shoes, a wool shirt, and an old slicker from his suitcase. He dressed hurriedly in the cold room.

When he entered the warm kitchen Doris Edwards was already there getting breakfast. She smiled at Dan and asked, "Did you have a good sleep?"

"Yes."

"Fine. As soon as you men finish milking, breakfast will be ready."

Outside the wind and rain bit into him. He hunched his shoulders against the storm and ran down the slippery hill, his slicker whipping against his legs. Inside the barn it was warm. The compressor was banging away. The cows were rattling their stanchions and busily licking up the grain in their mangers. Nipper sat on his tail in the aisle behind the cows, tongue hanging out, looking important. He gave Dan a long look, then turned his head away.

This morning Mr. Edwards showed Dan how to fork hay into the cow's mangers, after they'd finished their grain.

"Take about half a forkful," he explained, stabbing a pitch-fork into the mountain of loose hay. "Any more than this and they waste it. Then you shove it carefully into a corner of the manger, not the middle. That's where her head is and you might stick her in the eye and blind her. Get it in the corner, like this, and she'll reach it. Okay, you try it."

Dan plunged the fork into the hay. It went in the full length of the tines and he could not even budge the huge amount. He pulled the fork out halfway and lifted. Balancing it he stepped down to Bell's manger and stuffed it into a corner. Bell swung her head and ripped at the hay, jerking it toward her.

Mr. Edwards watched him do two more, then he nodded and returned to the milking. Dan went down the line feeding each cow. Ginger tossed her head at him but he was well beyond reach. Blossom licked his pants again. He stopped and patted her head, smiling faintly. He even fed Junior. The bull just glared at him out of mean red-rimmed eyes and rattled his chains.

Dawn was breaking wet and soggy over the distant hills when they finished and went in to breakfast.

Jennie was eating, her schoolbooks on the table beside her plate. She looked clean and scrubbed, her blonde hair shining under the kitchen light. She smiled at Dan and said, "I bet you never got up this early in the city."

"No," Dan said.

"Will you quit stalling, Jennie?" her mother said. "The bus will be here in a few minutes. Frank, Dan, sit down."

Breakfast was hot cereal, a pitcher of milk, bacon, eggs, and toast. This morning there was little talking at the table. Dan got the impression that breakfast was a meal to be gotten over with so the day's work could begin.

As soon as they finished, Mr. Edwards rose and pulled on his coat again. Jennie came from her room booted and coated, ready for school.

She followed them outside. The yellow schoolbus, loaded with students, was just pulling up at the head of the lane. Jennie ran carrying her books and lunch pail. Dan watched as she climbed aboard and the bus pulled into the road again. Jennie waved from a rear window. After a moment Dan lifted a hand.

Mr. Edwards said, "First thing now is to look at the baby chicks. Give them fresh mash and water, check the heat, and see if there are any dead or sick."

Nipper bounded off the porch and led the way down the mud-slick hill to the brooder house. He waited outside by the door when they went in.

The heat was all right. The chicks were not bunching up. They gave them fresh water and mash. There was one dead.

"What happened to it?" Dan asked.

"There's no teeth marks so it wasn't a rat," Mr. Edwards said. "It could have been trampled or smothered. It probably got sick during the night. There's no telling when they're so little."

Back at the barn they turned the cows into the pasture. Then Mr. Edwards carefully unfastened Junior's chains, threw open the stall door, and let him into the barn lot. Junior stomped about through the mud, shook his horns, and bellowed menacingly.

They washed and sterilized the milking equipment.

Then they took the pitchforks and began cleaning the barn. Nipper hunted up a pile of straw in a secluded corner, curled up, and went to sleep.

It took more than half the morning to clean all twenty stalls and mangers, haul in bales of fresh straw, break them open and spread a fresh layer in each stall. Mr. Edwards worked with the steady killing monotony of a machine and he seldom spoke. The only sounds were Junior's grumbling, the monotonous drum of rain on the tin roof, and Dan's own labored panting as he strove mightily to keep up with Mr. Edwards. But he could not. He lacked the man's strength and his knack of using leverage to lift. By the time they finished, his palms were sore and the muscles of his arms were jumping with fatigue.

"Now we can pitch down the hay for tonight's feeding," Mr. Edwards said and without a pause to rest he climbed the ladder through the trap door into the loft.

This was the hardest job of all. Mr. Edwards stood high on the mountain of hay, up near the peak of the barn, and pitched great forksful down to Dan. Dan dragged it to the trap door and shoved it through to the floor below.

Fine dust boiled up from the bone-dry hay, got in his mouth, eyes, and nostrils. He sneezed and coughed. His eyes watered. He could not handle as big a forkful as Mr. Edwards. The mound before him grew. The ache in his arms spread across his chest and shoulders and settled under his shoulder blades. Every muscle cried out for rest. And still the great forksful tumbled down with maddening regularity. Sweat ran in his eyes. He skinned out of his coat and tossed it aside.

31

He's doing it on purpose, Dan thought angrily. He's trying to show me I'm not good enough, just like he said.

Angrily he drove the fork too deep into the hay. He could not lift the load. He pulled the fork out halfway and left half the hay. He dragged this to the trap door, shoved it through, and ran back for more.

The soreness in his hands turned to fire. Then he discovered he had a dime-sized blister in each palm. He tried to ease the pressure on his hands but there was no way and he worked on doggedly. The blisters broke and there was blood on the fork handle. He changed his grip, trying to protect his palms. Then he could not handle the fork properly. He tried gripping with just his fingers but the fork turned over and he lost the load of hay. He was trying to find another grip when Mr. Edwards strode down off the mountain of hay and reached for his hand.

"Why didn't you say something?" he demanded almost angrily. "There's no sense letting this happen. I didn't think."

"It's all right." Dan pulled his hand away.

"It's not all right. You're going up to the house and let Doris put some disinfectant and tape on these hands. And get that new pair of canvas gloves off the shelf in the kitchen." He pushed Dan toward the ladder, "Get going, boy. And put on your raincoat," he added gruffly.

Doris Edwards scolded in a sympathetic voice as she doctored and bandaged his hands, "Why didn't you stop? That must have been terribly painful." And when Dan didn't answer, "You don't have to prove anything. Pitching hay isn't a life and death matter. Don't try to keep up with Frank. He's a grown man and toughened to this kind of work. . . . There, now, that ought to do it. Here's your gloves, and you leave that pitchfork alone the rest of the day."

"We're not through yet," Dan said.

"Frank can finish."

"No," Dan said.

Doris Edwards looked at him steadily. "Men!" she said. "They're all alike. The only difference between you and Frank is that he's older and therefore more stubborn. I don't know, maybe . . ." She shook her head and left the rest unsaid. "Go ahead, but be careful."

When Dan returned to the barn Mr. Edwards was still pitching hay out of the loft. He called down, "You put the grain in the mangers for tonight. One bucketful to a cow. After that, check the baby chicks. You know how. And gather the eggs."

None of these jobs required a pitchfork. When he left to go to the brooder house and laying house, Nipper rose from his straw bed and started to follow. Dan slipped out the door and slammed it in the dog's face.

At the brooder house the baby chicks were fine. He went on to the laying house. He found a number of hens on nests, but, by going about the egg gathering as purposefully as Jennie had, he was pecked only once.

When he finished, Mr. Edwards and Nipper were coming from the barn. It was time for lunch. Dan thought of all the work they'd done this morning and wondered what could possibly be left for the afternoon.

Mr. Edwards showed him as soon as they finished eating. "Well," he said, "let's see what the river has to offer."

Mystified, Dan followed him out beyond the barn and

across the pasture, head bent against the steady lash of the wind and rain. The pasture was spongy soft. Water oozed up around his feet with a sucking sound. They were heading toward the river, but before they were halfway there Dan's feet were soaked. Unmindful of the rain, Nipper trotted ahead, splashing through puddles and investigating every grass clump and brush patch. The big dog seemed to know where they were going.

Dan had never seen the Columbia anywhere but on its winding course between the cities of Vancouver and Portland. Here, he was surprised to discover, the river was an almost mile-wide sheet of swift-flowing water. Its surface was torn into whitecaps. As far as he could see the banks were lined with brush and trees and giant rocks.

They came to a backwater and there a half dozen pilings had been sunk into the riverbed, to form a line about a hundred feet long. A cable was fastened to the pilings and some twenty logs were attached to the cable by short chains, pieces of rope, and lengths of wire. An old, scarred, white cabin boat, with the name *Methuselah* printed crudely on the bow, was tied to one of the pilings.

"Jennie named her," Mr. Edwards said. He got hold of the rope, pulled the bow close to shore, and Nipper scrambled over the side. Mr. Edwards and Dan followed. The aft end of the cabin housed the old motor, the rest of the space served as the wheelhouse. Mr. Edwards said, "She's an old tub but she's stout; perfect for this sort of work."

"What work?" Dan asked.

"Salvage. There's a lot of logging going on back in the hills. They dump the logs into the river where they're made into big rafts. The rafts are then tied to the bank where they wait for a call to the sawmills. Sometimes there's a couple of hundred rafts tied up along the next twenty or thirty miles. A storm or high wind, or a boat coming too close and making waves, bounces logs out of the rafts and they float away. I've got a salvage license. I catch them with *Methuselah* and tie them up here. When I get a bunch they're auctioned off and I get sixty percent of the money for my work. Sometimes it pays off real well. I'd been counting on that extra money to build a new barn. But not at the rate we've been catching them in the past six months." He scowled. "There's been no storms or high winds or anything to bounce logs out of the rafts."

Mr. Edwards tried to start the old motor. It sputtered and coughed. He continued to grind on it, muttering, "Wish I understood gas engines. You know anything about 'em?"

"It sounds like bad plugs and points," Dan offered. "And it smells like your choke's stuck open and the carburetor's flooded, too."

"I remember now. They told me you were good with motors." He stepped away. "See if you can start it."

Dan checked the carburetor, found the choke stuck open, and closed it. While he waited for the flooded carburetor to clear he removed the distributor cap and inspected the points. "Points are bad," he said, "and you need a new rotor." He replaced the cap and tried the starter. On the third spin the motor sputtered unevenly to life. "It won't run much longer without repairs," Dan said.

"Think you can fix it?"

"I can try."

Mr. Edwards took the wheel and with no further words

they churned out into the broad bosom of the river. Nipper stationed himself in the bow, tail waving and tongue hanging out, grinning. Dan said, "He seems to like it."

Mr. Edwards nodded, "Like some dogs do a car. He goes crazy every time we spot a log and runs around like mad until I've got it tied up astern. I guess he thinks it's alive and we're catching it."

The old boat heeled over against the slam of the wind and rain. She dove into the whitecaps, digging deep. A sheet of spray fanned over the bow drenching Nipper, but he just shook himself and grinned. Against wind and current the limping motor found heavy going. They cruised slowly upriver for almost an hour. They passed an island several miles long and Mr. Edwards said, "Arrowhead Island. It splits the channel. This side is safe for a boat because it's wide and deep. The other side's narrow and shallow and swift as a millrace. Boatmen call it Suicide Run because it's almost certain death for a boat this size to try to get through."

They passed huge rafts moored to trees or rocks or pilings along the shore. They met several tugs towing rafts and they, too, were making slow progress against the storm and current. Finally Mr. Edwards cut across the river and they came booming with the current down the opposite side. They were opposite the tip of Arrowhead Island again when Nipper began dancing and barking wildly in the bow. Dan spotted the log bobbing through the whitecaps ahead of them. Mr. Edwards saw it, too. He advanced the throttle and made a run for it. Halfway there he abruptly turned away and cut the motor. The boat drifted with the current, the old motor idling unevenly. Dan looked at Mr. Edwards questioningly.

"It's heading into Suicide Run," he explained. "Too much risk. If this motor had been running right we'd have caught it. That sure is a nice one."

The log came opposite the tip of the island and it seemed to Dan he could see it shoot forward as it was caught in the swifter current. "Does Suicide Run empty into this main channel again at the far end of the island?" Dan asked. At Mr. Edwards' nod he added, "Couldn't we go down there and wait for the log and catch it when it comes out?"

"The chances of it coming out aren't good. The current in there can set it over against the bank. There's brush and rocks and shallow riffles for it to snag up on. Also we can't hang very long in that current at the lower end of the island and wait for the log to appear. It's too hard on the old motor."

"If we're going home we'll be passing by," Dan pointed out. "We could look."

"Okay, we'll give it a look."

They cruised the length of the island and cut across toward the tip where the swift water of Suicide Run emptied. Mr. Edwards slowed the motor and they lay against the current for several minutes looking about. Finally Mr. Edwards said, "I guess it hung up." He advanced the throttle again and swung the bow toward the distant bank and home.

At that moment Nipper began dancing and barking again. Dan's eyes followed the dog's and he saw the log bobbing through the chop a hundred yards away. "There it is!" he shouted and pointed.

"By golly, made it!" Mr. Edwards smiled suddenly. "This was your idea. You want to handle the boat? Come here." He pulled Dan to the wheel. "You've got two gears," he explained. "Forward and reverse. The motor itself acts as your brake. If you want to slow down your forward speed, throw it in reverse and race the motor. If you're backing up and want to stop, put it in forward. This lever is your throttle. All right, let's see you bring us alongside the log and hold the boat there while I snag it with the pike pole and make it fast astern." Mr. Edwards went outside, grabbed the pike pole off the cabin roof, and joined Nipper in the bow. He swung his arm motioning the boat forward.

Dan put the motor in gear and cranked the throttle. The boat moved forward against the current. Mr. Edwards waved his arm impatiently. Dan pulled the throttle open. *Methuselah* leaped ahead. Mr. Edwards stumbled backward from the bow. He twisted his head and shouted above the motor noise, "Slow down! Slow down!" They were rushing down upon the log with startling speed. For a few seconds all Dan could think of were brakes. Then he remembered. He spun the wheel, jerked the gearshift into reverse and yanked the throttle wide.

The boat struck with a crash. The bow tilted skyward as it climbed the log. *Methuselah* rocked sickeningly. Mr. Edwards was thrown against the pilothouse. The motor

The boat struck with a crash. The bow tilted skyward as it climbed the log.

roared. The reversed propeller bit into the water. *Methuselah* shot backward and the bow came down off the log with a great splash.

The next instant Mr. Edwards was in the pilothouse. He brushed Dan roughly aside, grabbed the wheel and closed the throttle. *Methuselah* stopped dead in the water.

Mr. Edwards went forward and leaned over the bow to inspect the damage. He returned grim faced.

"Is it bad?" Dan asked fearfully.

Mr. Edwards shook his head. "We're in luck this time. But one more like that will cave in the bow sure. Then I'll be permanently out of the log-salvaging business."

He put the motor in gear, eased the throttle open, and crept up beside the bobbing log. Nipper went wild with excitement again. He began dashing back and forth, barking at the top of his lungs. He charged into the pilothouse through one door and out the other. Then he leaned over the bow and kept up a steady barking at the log.

Mr. Edwards cut the motor, picked up the pike pole from the deck where he'd dropped it, stabbed it into the log, and led it to the stern where he secured it with a short length of chain that had a foot-long piece of metal shaped like a nail in one end. He drove the metal into the log with a sledge, then secured the opposite end to a cleat on the boat. He asked for no help.

The moment the log was made fast to the stern Nipper's frantic excitement disappeared.

Mr. Edwards returned to the cabin, took the wheel, and put the motor in gear. They angled across the river and headed for home with the log in tow. Neither of them spoke.

Dan put his hands carefully on the window ledge and looked out the side window. He had grabbed the wheel and gear shift lever too hard and had broken open the blisters. His palms were bleeding again. He gritted his teeth and endured the pain.

They saw no more logs and a half hour later they slipped into the calm backwater and eased up to the piling where Mr. Edwards made the boat fast.

They tied the log with the rest and Mr. Edwards scowled at the few he had gathered. "One log today," he grumbled to himself. "With this wind and rain we should have picked up half a dozen." He turned to Dan, "Do you still think you can fix that motor?"

"Yes," Dan said. "But it's going to take some new parts, like new plugs, points, and a distributor rotor. I don't know what else."

Mr. Edwards nodded. "Go ahead. There's tools in that tin box in the corner. I think there's a new rotor and points in there, too. Figure out what other parts you'll need and I'll get 'em. Nipper and I'll go up to the barn and work the rest of the afternoon."

The first thing Dan did was remove the canvas gloves and soak his hands in the cold river until the aching and burning stopped. Then he put the gloves on again and went to work on the distributor. He removed the old rotor and points. He found others in the tin box. They weren't new, but they looked good so he put them in. Then he tried the motor. It started easier and ran smoother, but it needed more work. He noticed the mooring line was slack. On impulse he removed his gloves, eased the motor in gear and carefully advanced the gas lever until the boat moved forward. He put it in reverse, felt the propeller bite into the water and stop the boat. He shut off the motor, smiling faintly. He had the feel of the boat now. And there were at least three notches of loose throttle on the gas lever. With gloves on and his sore hands he'd had no sense of touch back there in the river. He'd opened the throttle wide when he hadn't meant to. Try to explain that to Mr. Edwards, he thought bitterly.

He returned to work on the motor. He cleaned out the carburetor, blew out the gas line, and took the head off. He was enjoying himself working at something he knew, when a man splashed across the storm-washed pasture and climbed aboard. He was big and loose-jointed, with a pleasantly homely face and the broadest, thickest hands Dan had ever seen. He bent his tall head to enter the cabin. Once inside he seemed to fill the small space. He took off his hat, shook water from it, and said, "I'm Hank Simmons."

Dan carefully laid down the part he was holding, and suddenly all his enjoyment was gone. He knew who this man had to be.

Hank Simmons sat down on an upended box and looked out at the rain-drenched land, "Nasty day," he observed. "Few more like this and you'll need hip boots to cross that pasture."

"Yes," Dan said.

Hank Simmons looked at the old motor. "I see Frank's got you working on that already. He never did know beans about an engine. But put him two hundred feet in the air on a bridge structure and he's right at home."

Dan said, "You're my parole officer."

42

"Technically, yes." Hank Simmons smiled, "I'm hoping I can be your friend, too."

"I didn't expect to see you so soon."

"I had to come up this way so I thought I'd drop in, say 'hello' to my old friends, Frank and Doris, get acquainted with you, and try to answer any questions you might have."

Dan wasn't taken in. Behind the smile and friendly manner there was a very tough man. He didn't know how to talk to Hank Simmons or what he should say. Then he remembered Rocky's advice about going along with everything and making it easier for himself. After this day's happenings he was not interested in that advice. The anger that had been building since morning came out in a rush.

"Why send me up here? I'm no farm kid. I don't know a thing about cows and bulls and chickens and things. If I have to live with somebody else, why can't it be in the city where I belong?"

"Because that's where you got into trouble," Hank Simmons said calmly.

"I didn't steal that car. I didn't hold up that supermarket. You know how it was."

"You drove," Hank Simmons pointed out. "You ran with the gang. You had for months. The judge gave you a break because he was sure you weren't in on that job."

"Some break!"

"You'll see it is."

"I'll bet," Dan said sarcastically.

"Now about school," Hank Simmons went on, "spring term's started. It's going to take you a little time to get adjusted here. You might as well skip this term and concentrate on getting your feet on the ground, so to speak."

"You mean in the mud."

"I know it won't be easy for a boy with your background."

"I've already found that out. Are you the friend that helped Mrs. Edwards get me up here?"

Simmons nodded. "I've known them a long time. I was raised on a farm about twenty miles north of here. When Doris came to me with this idea last fall, I thought it was good. I know what a boy, the right boy, will mean to them. And I know what farm life with such a family can do for a boy. But we had to wait for the right boy to come along; one who could be paroled, and one that I felt the Edwards would like."

"Mrs. Edwards and Jennie are okay. I can get along with them fine. But not with Mr. Edwards."

"Frank's slow and he's careful, always has been. He's a fine man. Once you know him and he knows you you'll hit it off."

"That's not how I see it."

"How do you see it?"

"I see us getting along like a couple of stray alley cats. But I'm stuck here a whole year anyway."

"It's not that way at all."

"Tell me how it is."

Hank Simmons studied Dan soberly a long moment. He shook water from his hat brim, then he said quietly, "You're not stuck here at all if you really don't want to be."

"How so?"

"If you can't get along with the Edwards family, and

they can't get along with you, I'll have to find you another home."

"You're sure about that?"

"That's the way it works."

Dan almost trembled as elation surged through him. "All right, get me out of here," he said quickly.

"You'd better think about this pretty carefully," Simmons cautioned. "The judge gave you a break because he thought you deserved one."

"Give it to somebody else."

"You'd rather be at Hill View with the other four members of your gang, or at Halfway House with Rocky Nelson?" Simmons asked.

"They're my friends."

"Some friends."

"They're the only ones I've ever had."

"And they sold you out when they didn't tell you what was up that night. Especially that Rocky did. I'm betting he won't be at Halfway House more than a few weeks. He'll cause some trouble. At his age and with his record they'll ship him off to the big pen. Here, you're on a good, clean farm with some decent people."

"I'm in a mudhole with three complete strangers," Dan said.

Simmons shook his head. "You're disappointed. I can understand that. But you're looking at it all wrong."

"You would think so," Dan answered. "You were raised on a farm. I wasn't and I don't intend to be."

Simmons looked down at his muddy shoes and idly turned his hat in his big hands. Finally he said soberly, "I can find you another place to stay. That's no big problem. But I can promise you it won't be back in the city. And there's no guarantee it'll be as nice as this."

"You *would* call this nice."

"I would. But as you said, I was raised on a farm. You've got to give yourself a little time to get adjusted to it."

Dan looked out the door at the slanting rain, the soaked pasture swept now by a hard wind and dotted with rain pools. In the distance he could see the cows standing heads down, miserable. Beyond them was the old barn and laying house, and on the barren knoll the farmhouse, forlorn and lonely against the leaden sky. He thought of mud and biting wind and the utter darkness and stillness of the night. He thought of all the vacant miles back to the city. And he thought of the twenty cows and of Junior and Nipper. No place else would be worse. "I want out of here," he said to Hank Simmons. "Now!"

"Without giving it a try? You're a quitter?"

"Call me anything. I've given it all the try I'm going to."

"Made up your mind in less than a day, eh?"

"A lot less. I'll go back with you now."

Hank Simmons shook his head, "Not so fast! I've got to find another place for you. That takes a little time."

"How much?"

Hank Simmons shrugged. "Maybe a month. You're not the only boy I've got."

"All right," Dan agreed. "I'll be waiting."

"Just like that and you're through, eh?" Simmons asked. Dan nodded.

Hank Simmons just looked at Dan for a moment. Then

46

he sighed gustily and rose, dusted off his pants, and slapped his hat against his leg with an angry gesture. "All right, I'll get you out. I don't usually miss so far on a boy."

"You missed a mile this time."

"I sure did." Simmons voice was not friendly now. "Don't give Frank and Doris a bad time while you're here. I'll get you out as soon as I can. And don't say anything about leaving. I'll do that when the time comes." He started to leave, then stopped, head bent in the doorway. "You might like to know. They found your uncle. He's up at the State Hospital now, undergoing treatment as an alcoholic."

Dan watched the big man drop off the bow of the boat. His broad shoulders hunched against the drive of the rain as he splashed back across the pasture with his loose-jointed stride.

So he'd be leaving here in a few weeks after all. A great weight seemed to lift from his shoulders. He didn't want to think what the next place might be like. The important thing was he would be leaving here.

three

The knowledge that he would be gone soon from the farm made most of the annoyances bearable for Dan. But the routine of farm life never varied from that first morning. Dan's blistered hands healed in a couple of days. Then they toughened up and he discarded the gloves. More than half the work was done with a pitchfork, and by watching Mr. Edwards Dan soon learned to use his weight and leverage to advantage. He never lifted more than half the load Mr. Edwards could but now he did it with comparative ease. He still became tired, but not exhausted. The few minutes' break when he gathered the eggs and checked the baby chicks was enough to rest him so that he could finish the heavy work in the barn.

Mr. Edwards remained the same morose, nontalkative man. His silence, as they worked around the barn or rode the river looking for logs, kept reminding Dan that the man considered him incompetent, that he did not belong.

But Mr. Edwards' manner was different with the cattle. He was kind and gentle, his voice was soft and his hands caressing. "Milk cows are very sensitive," he explained to Dan. "They go down in their milk if you're rough and mean with them. It's good business to be gentle." But Dan knew there was more to it. Mr. Edwards loved the cows.

As for Nipper, Dan ignored the big black dog completely. At odd times when Dan did catch the dog watching him, he walked the other way, or turned his back. It seemed to work.

It didn't take Dan long to overhaul *Methuselah*'s motor. He ground the valves, put in new plugs, replaced part of the wiring that had become oil soaked and bare, tightened belts and bolts, and took up three notches of slack in the gas lever.

When they took the boat out the first time she bored smoothly into the current with power to spare. Mr. Edwards simply nodded and said, "That's fine."

Dan had hoped he'd get another chance to run *Methuselah* to prove to Mr. Edwards that he could. But the man stayed at the wheel and sent Dan up into the bow with the pike pole to spot for logs. Dan didn't like being up there with Nipper but he soon learned the dog wasn't interested in biting him. So they stood side by side and searched the swift-flowing water. The moment they spotted a floating log Nipper began barking at the top of his lungs and dashed wildly about the deck and in and out of the wheelhouse. Mr. Edwards would ease the boat up alongside the log where Dan would drive the needle-sharp pike pole into it, and lead it aft. There Mr. Edwards would take over and drive the spiked chain into the log and make it fast. Their catch remained very skimpy. But the time spent on the river was the happiest for Dan.

Dan got along well with Doris Edwards and Jennie. He couldn't break Jennie of calling him "Danny," and he finally gave up trying. Both women were anxious to make him feel at ease and did their best to include him in their conversations. But he could not join in their small talk. It always seemed to center around things and people strange to him, and he had no desire to learn about them.

Dan understood why Frank Edwards buried himself in the paper each evening and talked to no one. It was the only time he had to read. As for himself, he soon had read most of the magazines in the rack. He always ended his evenings by checking the baby chicks with Jennie before going up to his room. There he'd lie in bed and think about the gang.

One night he had the window partially open to air out the room and he heard the oddest noise. At first it seemed to come from somewhere down near the barn. A minute later it was repeated from another direction. Eerie, unreal, it floated on the silence and made his skin crawl. It came from nowhere and everywhere, and the night seemed bigger, emptier, more mysterious than ever. He stood it as long as he could. Then he dressed and went back downstairs. "There's a funny kind of sound out there," he said. "You think some animal or something might be bothering the cows or chickens?"

Mr. Edwards laid down the paper. "Let's go outside and listen."

They stood on the porch for several minutes, waiting. A fine mist was falling and water dripped steadily from the eaves. The barn and outbuildings were black bulks against the night. Thin streamers of fog drifted in from the river. There was not a star or trace of moon. Then it came again, a soft but carrying, "Whoooo, whoooo."

"Owls," Mr. Edwards said. "There's a pair of 'em. One sits on a rafter down at the barn, the other in that big tree about a hundred yards away. Every so often they start talking. Sometimes they'll keep it up for an hour."

"Oh," Dan said. But he didn't like the sound. It made him think of where he was and how far it was from home. When he went back upstairs he closed the window tight. It almost shut out the owls' talking.

He became familiar with all the activities on the farm. He learned to attach the cups of the milking machine to the cows' udders, and to clean and sterilize the machine after milking. The cows no longer worried him. He knew their peculiarities. Some liked to crowd him, some stood quietly while he worked around them, others stomped or moved about and had to be shoved over.

Ginger still swung her horns at him and he guessed she always would. Blossom licked his pants at every opportunity. Once when he came too near she almost tore his scalp off with her rough tongue. Of all the cows he liked her best. She was gentle and she always greeted him by making soft noises in her throat. She never tossed her head or seemed nervous. She waited patiently for her grain and hay.

17246

But Junior never changed. He glared out of red eyes, snorted, and rattled his chains. Dan just fed him. Mr. Edwards always let him out into the barn lot for exercise and then enticed him back in with grain. There were other things Dan could not adjust to, like the utter dark, and the night 'silence, the mud, and this never ending feeling of being in another world. But he looked forward to Doris Edwards' wonderful meals, Jennie's good-bye wave from the back of the school bus in the morning, and the final egg gathering and check of the baby chicks at night.

At last the rain stopped and the sun came out. Under its winter brilliance the valley lay spread out clear and shining all the way to the hills. It didn't look so forlorn and forbidding. The numerous rain pools were a sky-blue radiance, and under the soft winter sun the old farm buildings took on an aged mellow warmth. Sun shafts danced on the river's restless surface until Dan had to shade his eyes as they searched for logs. Hundreds of gulls planed in from the river and walked about the pasture, searching for worms and bugs which were attracted back to the top of the ground by the sun's warm rays. Off in the distance the cows' hides took on a golden sheen. Now and then one of them would suddenly kick up her heels and run a few clumsy, joyous steps because the miserable rain had stopped.

One night in the barn Jennie beckoned Dan up beside Ginger. She took his hand, pressed it against the cow's bulging side and whispered, "Push in." He did and felt a convulsive movement against his palm. "That's the calf," Jennie said, her eyes big.

He looked at her sharply to see if she was making fun of him.

"Honest," she said.

Dan pressed his hand against Ginger's side again, and the small thump struck his palm as if something had kicked.

Mr. Edwards came down the line of cows and asked, "Feel anything?"

"I felt something," Dan said.

Mr. Edwards put his big hand in the same spot and pushed. "Yep," he said, and Dan saw one of his rare smiles. "A pretty healthy kick."

After that Dan pressed his hand against Ginger's side every night and felt the kick. The knowledge that there was another life in there never ceased to amaze him.

A few days later Mr. Edwards said, "It's time to move Ginger into the maternity ward."

The maternity ward was a box stall down at the end of the barn beside Junior. They put a foot of straw on the floor and turned her in. "We'll have to watch her close," Mr. Edwards said as Ginger inspected her new quarters. "She could get milk fever."

"What's that?"

"A sickness that only a highly bred animal, a heavy milker such as Ginger, gets. During the months that she gives milk, her calf is also growing inside her. Both sap her strength and deplete her blood of vital minerals that she needs to live. These cows aren't always strong enough for natural birth and recovery. If they don't get help quick they'll die in a few hours."

"How can you tell if she's got milk fever?"

"When it's time for the calf to be born she'll be too weak to get up and there'll be a bow in her neck that she can't straighten. The bow will feel hard as a rock."

"What do you do?"

"I call the vet. He comes out and gives her a shot in the jugular vein. That shot replaces the minerals in her blood that have become low."

"Then she will be all right?"

"She'll be fine. It's not too serious, if she gets that shot in time. That's why we've got to watch her closely. I'd hate to lose Ginger. She's a valuable animal."

Dan thought later that while Mr. Edwards had been telling him about Ginger he'd glimpsed a different man, one who could be friendly and warm.

I guess, Dan decided, I'd just have to know a lot about cows to get along with him. But I won't be here long enough to learn that.

They watched Ginger closely for the next two days, but nothing happened. Noon of the third day Doris Edwards said at lunch, "Frank, have you forgotten that tonight's the milk co-op meeting and the election of officers? As chairman you've got to be there."

"So do you. You're recording secretary. Don't worry, we'll go."

"What about Ginger?"

Mr. Edwards shrugged. "Nothing's happening. If you remember she ran over her time almost three days with her last calf. She's going to do it again, sure. We can all go. She'll be all right."

"I'd rather stay here," Dan said.

Mr. Edwards said, "You'll get to meet some of the neighborhood people."

Dan shook his head.

"I think Dan's right," Doris Edwards said. "There's plenty of time to meet people. This will be an awfully dull meeting. I wish Jennie didn't have to go to help wait tables." She smiled at Dan, "You can keep the fire up and look in on Ginger once in a while."

"Suppose something starts to happen while you're gone?"

"We'll look in on her the last minute before we leave," Mr. Edwards said. "If she's all right then, she'll be okay till we return. This meeting will only be three or four hours."

During the milking that night when Dan went in to grain her, Ginger was lying in the middle of the stall, her legs tucked neatly under her. Dan passed close and she suddenly lunged at him with her horns. He jumped aside, dumped the grain in her box and went out.

Mr. Edwards was hooking the milking machine to a pair of cows and asked, "How's Ginger?"

"She tried to jab me with her horns."

"Then she's all right."

The milking finished, they hurried through supper and washed the dishes. By that time it was getting late and all three of the Edwardses rushed about getting ready to leave.

They were hurrying into the car when Mr. Edwards said, "Darn! I forgot to check Ginger again."

"You'll get your suit and shoes all muddy going down there now," Doris Edwards said. "Dan, you check her. We'll wait."

Dan ran down to the barn, snapped on the light and found Ginger lying in the same spot. She threw up her head and looked at him, her eyes shining like bits of glass.

"You don't hook me this time," Dan said. He snapped off the light and ran out.

"She's just like she was," he told Mr. Edwards.

"Not threshing around or anything?"

"She's still lying there. All she did was look at me."

Mr. Edwards nodded and started the car, "Three days over again," he predicted. "Just like I figured."

"Don't forget to look at the baby chicks," Jennie called, as the car ran down the lane.

Dan started into the house and Nipper trotted up to crowd in with him. "Not with me, you don't." Dan slammed the door before the dog could get in.

He wandered restlessly about the house. He wished they had television, but there wasn't a chance for it out here in the country without a cable. He rummaged through a stack of old magazines and found a story about hunting wolves in the north. He settled down to read it.

The kitchen clock was striking nine when he finished. He remembered the baby chicks, got into his coat, took the flashlight and went out. Nipper rose from the porch and started to follow. Dan stopped and faced the dog. He pointed at the porch and said sternly, "Lie down, Nipper. Lie down."

Nipper seemed to understand. He returned to the porch and curled up near the door.

It was comfortably warm in the brooder house. Dan raised the door and peeked under the brooder. The baby chicks were scattered out and resting. He dropped the door and was about to leave when he saw the rat. He found the hammer on the ledge and advanced. The rat rushed about trying to escape. Dan crouched, spread his arms and drove the rat into a corner. He killed it with the first swing. He went out, closed the door carefully, tossed the dead rat into a hole, and kicked dirt over it.

As long as he was down here he might as well check Ginger again.

She lay in exactly the same spot and gave him the same glassy-eyed stare. She moved a little, uttered a deep, gusty sigh, and lay still again. Dan turned out the light and started for the house. Halfway up the hill he stopped. Something about Ginger kept nagging at the back of his mind. Then he had it. She hadn't moved from that one position for hours, and he'd never seen that glassy shine in her eyes before tonight. He returned to the barn.

He turned on the lights and stood outside her stall studying her. She had kicked the straw away until it was almost down to the concrete. She might have been trying to get up. He unlatched the gate, stepped into the stall and walked around her. Her breathing seemed heavier. He got behind her, grabbed her tail, bent it toward her spine and pulled to get her up. Ginger heaved mightily, almost reached her knees, then fell back with an explosive sigh. Dan knew then she hadn't tried to hook him when he'd grained her earlier. She'd been trying to get up and she couldn't make it, even then. That odd shine in her eyes was pain. What was the other thing Mr. Edwards had said to look for? A bow in her neck that would be hard.

Her neck had a bow. He moved to her opposite side and tried to attract her attention so she'd turn her head. He put

57

his hand on her head expecting her to toss it up as always. She didn't. Dan stepped close then and ran his hand down her neck. It was hard as rock. She had milk fever and she'd probably had it for hours. He didn't like those deep, sighing sounds, and now that he was here she kept trying to move. She wanted to get up. Ginger had been sick more than four hours that Dan knew of.

And Mr. Edwards had said that if she didn't get help quick she'd die in a matter of hours. The Edwardses wouldn't be home until round midnight. He wondered if she could live that long. Maybe he could telephone that co-op place and tell them. He turned out the light and ran up the hill to the house.

Dan found the Valley Co-op listed in the telephone book and called the number. The phone rang and rang. Finally he hung up. Either no one was there or the phone was in another part of the building.

He tried to think what to do next. Mr. Edwards had said that he'd call the vet. Dan hunted through the book again and found listed a Dr. Andresen, veterinarian. He was the only veterinarian in the book so Dan called him.

Again the phone rang and rang. He was about to hang up when a sleepy voice said, "Dr. Andresen."

Dan told him who he was and explained about Ginger.

"So you're the new boy at the Edwardses'," Dr. Andresen said. "Yes, I take care of Frank's cattle. How long's she been down? About four hours you think. I'll be right over. Meet me at the barn."

Dan hung up, his heart hammering. The doctor's quick, businesslike voice had sent a wave of impending disaster washing over him. Why hadn't he asked if there was anything he could do to get ready? The vet'd probably need hot water. They could get that at the milk house. He'd likely need some clean cloths, some hand towels.

Dan's mother had once had a rag bag. He searched hurriedly through closets but found none. He went to the kitchen and got a dozen dish towels. From the bathroom he took two of Mrs. Edwards' best bath towels. Carrying these Dan ran down to the barn. Nipper followed him off the porch but was careful to keep a respectful distance. Dan got a bucket for hot water, then put it and the towels beside the manger. Now there was nothing to do but wait.

Nipper whined and scratched at the barn door. He knew something unusual was happening.

Dan went into the stall and looked at Ginger again. She moved her legs and heaved upward feebly, then she lay back and expelled her breath with a tired sigh. She seemed weaker than she'd been a few minutes ago. Dan patted her head and ran his hand down the hard bow of her neck.

So, Ginger had tried to hook him a few times! But now she was sick. She might die. She needed help desperately, and there was nothing he could do. He felt terribly sorry for her. "Just take it easy," he told her gently. "The doctor'll be here soon and then it'll be all right." Dan put his hand on her neck again. She felt cold. He found some grain sacks and spread them carefully over her. Then he settled down to wait.

The minutes dragged. He went to the barn door and looked up toward the house and the lane. There was no dark bulk of a car there; no headlights probed the lane. Nipper backed away from the door when Dan opened it. He closed it in the dog's face and returned to Ginger.

59

He patted Ginger and talked to her. He ran a hand under the sacks to see if she was getting warmed. She wasn't. Ginger lifted her nose and smelled of him. She seemed to be glad he was near.

Dan's anxiety increased. It seemed he could see Ginger weakening before his eyes. He returned to the door for another look. He had made two more trips and was back squatting beside Ginger, petting and talking to her, when the barn door opened. A man came in carrying an old leather bag.

Dan took one look at the man and was bitterly disappointed. He didn't know what he expected Dr. Andresen, veterinarian, to look like. But not like this. This man was short and fat. He wore an old cloth jacket, overalls, and a shapeless, weather-stained hat. He was chewing on a stub of cigar that had never been lit. Dr. Andresen nodded at Dan, put the bag on the floor and glanced at Ginger. "Fine! You covered her up. That's important." His voice was matter of fact and dry as rustling straw. He noticed the bucket for warm water and the little pile of towels. He nodded. "Good," he said.

"Does she have milk fever?" Dan asked.

"Of course." Dr. Andresen didn't even look at Ginger. "Suppose you fill that bucket with warm water."

When Dan returned with the water Dr. Andresen had pulled off his jacket and opened the old leather bag to disclose an array of shining instruments and an assortment of bottles, huge pills, capsules, and rolls of bandages. He said around the cigar, "I'll need some help to give her this shot." He took a bottle of medicine from the bag, attached a short tube and handed it to Dan. "Hold this up and be careful with it."

Dr. Andresen knelt beside Ginger, felt along her neck, found the jugular vein and thrust the needle in full length. "Now hold the bottle high so the liquid can feed down into her."

Dan watched fascinated as the liquid ran down the tube a drop at a time and disappeared into Ginger's neck. So that contained the minerals Mr. Edwards had told him a cow might become low in. The vet was now replacing them.

Finally the bottle was empty, and Dr. Andresen pulled out the needle. "Now we wait a few minutes to let that medicine take effect," he said.

"How soon can she get up?"

"It varies from a few minutes to half an hour or so."

They sat side by side against the wall of the stall, watched Ginger, and waited. Dr. Andresen chewed on the unlit cigar and asked, "How do you like living here?"

Dan hedged. "I'm from the city."

"Don't like it," Dr. Andresen said. "Well, maybe you'll get to like it, maybe you won't. These are fine people and Frank's a good dairyman. I've known him for years. Needs a new up-to-date barn, though." They sat silent for several minutes, then Dr. Andresen got up and felt of Ginger. He sat down again and they waited. It was quiet in the barn. Junior rattled his chains and snorted. A stanchion made a clashing of metal as a cow lay down.

Ginger had stopped moving her legs and trying to heave herself upward. She no longer uttered those deep sighs. She lay quiet and seemed to be resting.

61

After a few more minutes Dr. Andresen walked around Ginger studying her critically. Finally he began rolling up his sleeves, exposing short, muscular forearms. "Take off your coat and roll up your sleeves," he said to Dan.

Dan slipped out of his coat, and an odd feeling of apprehension began to tighten his stomach. "What're we going to do?"

"That calf is trying to be born but the cow's still too weak. We've got to help her. We're going to take the calf."

"I've never done this," Dan burst out. "I don't know what to do."

"You'll do exactly as I tell you." Dr. Andresen extracted a length of small chain from his bag. "Now roll up those sleeves."

The next few minutes were like a dream to Dan. Dr. Andresen talked around the unlit cigar stub as he worked over Ginger. And Ginger lay perfectly still as if she knew he was trying to help her. "I've got to fasten this chain around the calf's front feet," he explained. "Then when Ginger pushes, we pull and help her, and the calf gets born." After a minute he stood up. "All right. We're ready. Get a good hold on this chain with me. When she strains we pull. And don't yank," he warned. "Just a good steady pull. I'll say when. Get ready."

Dan braced his feet and clutched the chain with sweaty hands. He kept his eyes glued to Ginger. He had the feeling she was gathering this new-found strength she'd got from the bottle for one great effort. He saw her body surge powerfully upward.

Dr. Andresen said sharply, "Now!"

They both leaned into the chain and pulled. Dan was

surprised at how hard they had to pull. Then suddenly there was the calf lying in the straw at their feet.

For a sick moment Dan thought the calf was dead. Then its pink nose wrinkled and its sides heaved as the first gush of fresh air rushed into its lungs. Its small head raised feebly, and the biggest, clearest eyes Dan had ever seen blinked at the strange new world into which the calf had so suddenly been born.

"A nice little heifer," Dr. Andresen observed. "Take her hind legs. This cow's going to get up in a minute. We don't want her stepping on her calf."

They laid the calf in the straw a few feet off and Dr. Andresen said, "Take those sacks off the cow and rub the calf down. We've got to dry her off or she'll catch cold."

Dan had gone over the calf once with the sacks when Ginger scrambled to her feet. She stood trembling violently. Then the trembling passed and she came toward Dan, head down making soft sounds in her throat. Dan feared she would not understand his attentions toward her baby and would swing her horns at him as she had so often. He started to scramble out of her way. But Ginger paid no attention to him. She lowered her head beside him, began licking the calf, and the soft sounds kept murmuring in her throat. The calf lifted its head as if it understood and Ginger licked its face dry.

Dan sat back on his heels and marveled. This was what had been kicking his palm for days. This was why Ginger had got sick, why she had gone dry, and why she would give milk again. A minute ago there'd been only Ginger. Now there were two. And he'd helped bring this new life into the world. He had the odd feeling that he'd taken part in some great event. And yet it was so commonplace that Dr. Andresen could go on chewing on his cigar unconcernedly while he washed and dried his arms and replaced the instruments in the old leather bag.

"We'll let Ginger clean her up good," he said. "Then we'll get the calf up and help her have a drink of milk. I want to be sure she gets a good meal of this first milk. It's rich in everything she needs to give her a flying start."

A few minutes later they lifted the calf between them. Ginger stood quietly, only turning her head to be sure all was going well. It took a bit of maneuvering to get the calf in the proper position but once there, it knew exactly what to do. It began sucking noisily.

"Is she getting anything?" Dan asked.

Dr. Andresen nodded and jerked his head at the calf's tail which was beginning to swing sharply back and forth. "Dead giveaway," he said.

They finished and were letting the calf lie down again when the barn door opened. All three Edwardses hurried in.

"We found Doc's car up at the house," Mr. Edwards explained. "How's Ginger?"

"All right now," Dr. Andresen slipped into his old jacket and picked up his bag. "We had to give her a shot and take the calf. If the boy hadn't called me she'd probably be dead now."

Mr. Edwards shook his head, "I was so sure she'd run over, like last time."

"A little heifer," Doris Edwards said. "I'm glad."

A minute ago there'd been only Ginger. Now there were two.

64

"She's beautiful," Jennie said happily. "Just beautiful."

Dan saw Mrs. Edwards looking at the pile of dish towels and bath towels he'd brought down. He said, "I thought we might need some rags or something. I couldn't find any so I brought these. But we didn't have to use them."

"I'm glad you got them," she said. "You were really busy, weren't you?"

"He had everything ready when I got here," Dr. Andresen said. "I went right to work."

They all trooped out of the barn and up the hill to the house. Dr. Andresen said, "Better look in on Ginger a couple of times tonight, Frank. She might need another shot." He looked at Dan, then removed the cigar from his mouth and said, "We had quite an evening. Eh, boy?" Then he got into his car, drove down the lane and out onto the highway.

They filed into the kitchen and Jennie said, "I brought you some cake, Danny."

"I can eat some," Dan said. "I'm hungry."

"I'll bet you're half starved," Doris Edwards said and headed for the refrigerator.

"For Pete's sake get the boy something to eat," Mr. Edwards said. "He's put in practically another full day. We had some roast left over from supper. How about a sandwich to go with that cake, Dan? And some milk? Jennie, bring me the carving knife. Doris, where's that roast?"

While Dan stuffed himself with cake, a sandwich of roast beef, and several glasses of milk, the three Edwardses sat across the table insisting they should hear everything that had happened during the evening.

"Everything?" Dan asked.

"From the minute we drove out of the yard." Mr. Edwards leaned his elbows on the table and waited intently.

"Well," Dan took a huge bite of cake and washed it down with half a glass of milk.

Doris Edwards immediately refilled the glass.

"After you left I went inside and read an article about hunting wolves in the north. It was pretty good—"

Mr. Edwards could wait no longer. "When did you first suspect something was wrong with Ginger?"

"When I checked the baby chicks at nine. I found a rat in there," he told Jennie. "I killed it. It didn't get any chicks." He explained how he'd looked in on Ginger, then became suspicious when she hadn't moved. "You'd have spotted it at milking time," he said to Mr. Edwards.

"Maybe not. Sometimes it's hard to detect at first. Anyway, I thought she'd go over three days again. Remember?"

"Well," Dan continued, "I called that co-op number but nobody answered."

"That's the office," Doris Edwards said. "This meeting was held downtown."

"Then I called the only veterinary listed in that little blue book you've got. And that's about all. Dr. Andresen did the rest."

"And you helped him," Mr. Edwards said. "I'd say that was quite a lot. You handled it like a real experienced dairyman."

"Gosh!" Jennie said, "I'd have been scared Ginger would die before Doc got here."

"I was," Dan said, "and I couldn't think of a thing to do to help her."

67

"Seems to me you did just about everything," Doris Edwards said.

"What're you going to name the calf?" Mr. Edwards asked.

"Me name her?" Dan asked surprised.

"You know anybody that's got a better right?" Mr. Edwards demanded.

Dan thought hard. Then he looked at Jennie and began to smile. "You said she was beautiful. Let's call her Beauty."

"Beauty she is," Mr. Edwards said.

Jennie clasped her hands, her eyes shining, "I love it."

"So do I," Doris Edwards said. The clock began striking and she glanced up, "Why, it's midnight! Jennie, you get to bed. There's school tomorrow."

"I'd better check Ginger again," Dan said. "Doc wanted Beauty to get plenty of that first milk."

"I'll do that," Mr. Edwards heaved up from the table. He stood tall and lean as he looked down at Dan. All reserve and suspicion were gone from his gray eyes. "But for you we'd have lost Ginger and Beauty," he said gravely. "Losing them would have been an awful setback for us."

"Somebody would have stayed tonight," Dan said.

"No, we'd all have gone. I was so sure she'd run over again." Mr. Edwards slipped into his coat, "You sleep in tomorrow morning. I'll check the baby chicks again, too."

"Dr. Andresen said we should check Ginger a couple of times during the night," Dan reminded him. "She might need another shot."

"I'll take care of that, too."

"You're sure you can handle Beauty alone?" Dan asked.

"Stop worrying. I'll take good care of your calf." Mr. Edwards smiled at Dan and the boy found himself smiling back. Then Mr. Edwards went out and closed the door.

Dan finished the last bite of sandwich and rose. Doris Edwards said, "Dan."

"What?"

"You did fine. Just fine."

"I really was scared Ginger might die."

She shook her head, her brown eyes very bright, "Thanks to you she didn't. Good night."

Up in his room Dan undressed, cracked the window open for fresh air, and crawled into bed. He was still wide awake. He lay there and looked out the window. He could see a patch of night sky, some stars, and the point of a thin moon. The sky didn't seem as dark as it had that first night here. It had been raining that night. But spring's not far away, either, he thought. Days are getting longer.

Then he heard that eerie, unreal sound again coming from the direction of the barn. He listened, and there was a short silence. Then it was repeated. This time it came from the old maple tree a hundred or so yards to the left of the barn. It was soft and somehow melodious, and a part of the magic and the mystery of this night.

He folded his hands behind his head and smiled in the darkness. The owls were talking again.

four

The days following the birth of Beauty were busy ones for Dan.

The very next morning, as they stood leaning over the top plank of the box stall looking in at Ginger and Beauty lying side by side, Mr. Edwards said, "How'd you like to take over raising her: feed her, wean her, take complete care of her?"

Dan looked at Beauty curled up in the straw, head up, pink nose wrinkling as she breathed. Her big liquid eyes were fringed by the longest lashes he'd ever seen. His first reaction was to say, "I can't. I wouldn't know what to do." Then he thought of last night and how he'd helped Dr. Andresen deliver Beauty and save Ginger's life. Such an excuse sounded foolish. He asked, "Do you mean it?"

"You helped bring her into the world," Mr. Edwards pointed out. "This is no time to quit—with the job only half done. Now you have to make her into a well-behaved cow. The two of you can grow and learn together."

"What would I do?" Dan asked.

"We'll leave Ginger in the stall with her today and tonight. Tomorrow morning you make sure Beauty gets a good feeding of milk, then turn Ginger out with the rest of the cows so she can get some green feed and exercise. She'll become lonesome for her calf in a couple of hours and will be up here at the gate bawling and waiting. At noon you let her in again and see that Beauty has another good feeding. Then turn Ginger out for the afternoon. At night we'll let her in and leave her with the calf all night. We'll do that every day for a while."

So Dan took over the raising of Beauty and, in so doing, for the next few days he cared for Ginger, too. He was busier than he'd ever been in his life before.

After Dan turned Ginger into the pasture each morning he checked the baby chicks. The heat was gradually being lowered now, because the first tiny feathers were sprouting on the chicks' wings and tails. Then he returned to the barn and worked with Mr. Edwards. Once during the forenoon Dan went to the laying house and gathered the first eggs laid. By the time all that was finished it was noon and Ginger was bawling at the gate to get in to Beauty. Dan put her in, let Beauty get her fill, and turned Ginger out again.

Their afternoons were spent on the river. Mr. Edwards still ran the boat and Dan was up in the bow, pike pole in hand, looking for logs with Nipper. He hoped Mr. Edwards would give him another chance to operate the boat. He could handle it now. But day after day Mr. Edwards remained at the wheel. Dan hinted only once. A floating stump had drifted into the backwater blocking their exit. Mr. Edwards was out pushing it away with the pike pole and Dan called, "You want me to back the boat out?"

Mr. Edwards shook his head, "I'll do it in a minute." Dan never hinted again.

Their catches remained disappointingly few.

The fourth night, when they started to let in the cows Mr. Edwards said, "This'll be Ginger's ninth milking since Beauty was born. Her milk's good for human consumption now. Turn her into the stanchion."

"It wasn't good before?" Dan asked surprised.

"No. The first milkings are thick and feverish, don't even taste like milk. But they're rich in the things a calf needs. It takes nine milkings after a calf's birth before the milk is back to normal. So tonight we start weaning Beauty."

They milked Ginger out, then put several quarts of her milk into a sterilized pail and went into the stall with the calf. Beauty looked about anxiously for Ginger and began to bleat. "Now, she has to learn to drink and not nurse," Mr. Edwards said. "That's going to take some time and patience. She hasn't had any milk since noon so she's extra hungry tonight. Hold the pail tight in one hand and let her suck a finger of your other hand. When she's sucking, lower your hand into the milk and she'll suck the milk into her mouth around your finger. All right, try it."

Dan held the bucket firmly and offered a finger to Beauty. She grabbed it in her mouth and sucked greedily. He lowered his hand slowly into the milk and her head followed. She blew and sucked noisily and stamped her small feet. It was a wonderful sensation having her soft lips pulling at his finger. Her short tail began to switch back and forth. She closed her eyes blissfully and the contents of the pail began to lower.

Mr. Edwards said, "Now slowly ease your finger out of her mouth and hold it against her nose so she'll know it's still there. If she quits sucking or jerks her head up, put your finger in her mouth again and start over."

Dan eased his finger out and held it next to her lips. Beauty took a couple of sucks, then she snorted and jerked her head up, spewing milk. Dan shoved his finger in her mouth again and lowered it into the milk. She began drinking. He waited until she was sucking happily, then eased his finger out once more and held it against her nose close to her lips. She went on drinking.

Dan looked up and grinned. At that moment Beauty missed his finger and belted the pail with all her strength. He hadn't thought she was so strong and he wasn't well braced. He stumbled back a step, tangled in his own feet, and went over backward. The milk cascaded over him. Beauty rammed her head against his chest and began sucking eagerly on his soaked shirt.

It was the first time Dan had ever heard Mr. Edwards laugh outright. "First lesson," he said, "and this time you learned, too. Let's get some more milk."

Beauty learned fast. Within three days she would drink the pail dry as long as Dan held his finger on her nose. By the end of the week even that wasn't necessary. But she never got over butting the pail unexpectedly. Now, however, Dan was braced and ready for her. "A week," he bragged to Mr. Edwards, "and she can drink as well as any cow. I'll bet you never had a calf that did it any faster."

"She's intelligent," Mr. Edwards agreed. "She should make a good milker. I'd guess not less than a five-gallon cow." He folded his arms on the top rail of the stall and said thoughtfully, "When she comes in, her five gallons will supply ten families with two quarts of milk every day. Ever think of that?"

Dan did some quick arithmetic and said, "Jennie told me we get about eighty gallons a day from the herd. That'd take care of one hundred and sixty families."

"Nothing wrong with that arithmetic," Mr. Edwards smiled.

Dan thought about that amazing fact as he stroked Beauty's silken neck. He'd never thought about where the food came from. It was always on counters and shelves in the store. Of course someone had to milk cows, raise pigs and chickens, and harvest great fields of vegetables and grains. He gave Beauty a couple of final pats and said, "You'd better get big in a hurry. You've got ten families to feed." Beauty bobbed her head up and down, then rammed it into his stomach and waited for him to push back. He accommodated her and she immediately pushed again, testing her young strength.

Dan took his responsibility seriously, and the wonder of the calf's existence never left him. He'd recall pressing his hand against Ginger's side and feeling the kick, and of helping Dr. Andresen with the birth. Then he'd pet Beauty, scratch her ears, and let her small, hard head butt him, and be amazed all over again. The fact that the whole family called Beauty his calf pleased him.

Dan began checking the baby chicks alone at night so Jennie wouldn't have to go out in the rain again. But he had another and more important reason. He could look in on Beauty once more and visit with her when no one else was around. She always bleated a welcome as he entered the stall and sat down in the straw to pet her and talk to her. She'd suck at his pants or his shirt and he'd push her head aside and scold, "Stop that. You can drink now just like any cow. And don't try to kid me. You're not hungry. You had a big feed tonight. Why your stomach's as tight as a drum yet." Sometimes he'd lie beside her for a few minutes, an arm over her neck, his head close to hers and they'd listen to the steady drum of rain on the roof. He could feel the steady beat of her heart beneath his hand and the smoothness of her hide. When she raised her head to sniff at him her breath was soft and sweet against his cheek. One night he fell sound asleep lying there. Mr. Edwards finally came out and woke him an hour later. "I was afraid something might have happened," he said.

"She sort of likes having me around," Dan explained sheepishly, rubbing his eyes.

"I know," Mr. Edwards agreed. "Animals get to know and trust you, and they'll leave their own kind to be with you."

Dan left the stall and Beauty lifted her head and bleated after him.

"Quit acting like I'm going away forever," Dan said. "I'll be back in the morning."

"That's the way she bosses you around," Mr. Edwards smiled.

Dan thought about that. "I guess you're right. Is that bad?"

"There's people that'll tell you it is, but they're not good dairymen. I've got twenty bosses myself." When Dan looked puzzled he explained, "We need a new house. Ours is old and drafty and there's nothing modern about it. I know Doris wants one and I'd like to give it to her. But we need a new barn, too, so we can go Grade A and get the best out of our milk cows. So the house has to wait. It's always been that way with good farmers. Luckily most of their families understand."

Dan was surprised how fast Beauty grew and gained strength. Soon she was big and strong enough to be let out into the pasture with the cows for a few hours on sunny afternoons.

"But won't she try to nurse again?" Dan asked.

"She might, even though she is weaned," Mr. Edwards agreed. "But if she does, Ginger won't let her. Ginger is also weaned away from her calf to the extent that she won't let her nurse. She'll walk away from Beauty or kick at her to warn her off. She did with her calf last year."

"What about the other cows?"

"They'll run her off, all but Blossom. She's friendly and gentle. She'd let Beauty nurse but Blossom's dry, so the calf's stymied there."

The first time Beauty was reluctant to leave the security of her box stall, and Dan had to put a rope on her and pull her out with all four legs braced. "Come on," he panted, "you don't want to spend all your life in a box stall. There's a lot of world out here."

Once out in the pasture she was startled at this huge

land and stood head up, sniffing, big liquid eyes trying to take it all in. She smelled of the half-dead grass and snorted and stamped her small feet in the soft earth. Suddenly she kicked up her heels and, with her tail sticking straight up, went galloping awkwardly across the pasture in a great circle. It was the first time she had ever run and her spindly legs flailed out in all directions. She stumbled once and skidded to her knees, then she was up again, running as hard as ever. She returned to Dan snorting and panting. She rammed her hard little head against him and waited for him to scratch her ears and push against her. He did, and for a few seconds they had a pushing match. She turned abruptly and went galloping crazily across the pasture toward the distant cows, bleating at the top of her lungs.

Ginger met her and began smelling over her. Other cows came to investigate but Ginger's sharp horns ran them off. Blossom approached and touched noses with Beauty. Ginger watched and didn't try to run her away.

Beauty hadn't forgotten about nursing and soon went to her mother. Ginger walked away and when the calf followed the cow swung her head and kicked at her. It went just as Mr. Edwards had said it would. Beauty tried them all and was rebuffed until she came to Blossom. Blossom stood quietly, but Beauty found nothing there. After trying for a few seconds she gave up. In another minute Ginger and Blossom stood side by side licking the contented calf. Then the three went off together.

Dan smiled and returned to the barn.

It was the week after they'd first let Beauty into the pasture that Hank Simmons returned. It was another fine day with the warm winter sun beating down. Dan and Mr. Edwards were crossing the pasture toward the barn from another fruitless search on the river, when Simmons' long figure swung toward them with his loose-jointed stride. Simmons shook hands with each of them. "Hello, Dan. Frank. Nice weather." He removed his hat and looked up at the cloudless sky. "We generally get two or three weeks of this every winter and here it is again."

"Winter's getting close to the end," Mr. Edwards said. "I hope this warm weather don't hold too long. We need it cool so that big snowpack in the mountains will melt slowly. Weather too hot, too early, would make a big, fast runoff, and this river would be something to see."

"It could get pretty wild," Simmons agreed. "Has it risen any yet?"

"It's up a couple of feet. If it turns cool it'll go down again."

"That dike up at the Narrows ought to help."

"It will if the spring freshet doesn't get too high."

Hank Simmons spotted Beauty off with the cows and said, "Nice-looking little heifer. Isn't she a new addition?"

"Dan's heifer," Mr. Edwards said.

"Oh?" Hank Simmons looked at Mr. Edwards, then at Dan.

"Dan can tell you all about it," Mr. Edwards said. "It's quite a story. I'm going up and knock down some more hay for tonight. See you later."

They watched Mr. Edwards go on to the barn. Then Hank Simmons asked, "What's this about your heifer?"

"Beauty's not mine really," Dan explained as they

78

walked toward the grazing cows. "I helped the vet when she was born and the Edwardses just say that now."

"The cow had trouble?"

"Yes. That's her mother, Ginger. She had milk fever." Dan went up to Ginger and patted her neck. Ginger looked around at him, then moved off in search of a green tuft of grass.

A cow moved toward Dan and Simmons said, "Looks like there's going to be another addition pretty soon."

"This is Blossom." Dan put his arm around her neck. "She's a real baby. She's dry now. Her calf is due in about a month." Blossom licked at Dan's pants and sniffed at his face. Then she wandered off following Ginger.

"Think her calf will be as good as Ginger's?"

"Should be. They're both purebreds and Junior's the sire. I just hope she doesn't get milk fever, too."

Beauty rammed her small head against Dan from behind. Dan turned and patted her, and she promptly pushed against him testing her strength. He shoved back, and her front feet began to dance in anticipation of a game.

Hank Simmons smiled, watching him. "She's only a couple of weeks old, isn't she?"

"That's right. I never thought she'd get strong this fast the night she was born. I didn't even think she was going to live." Dan shoved Beauty away and looked at Hank Simmons. "Did you ever help take a calf?" he asked.

"No. I've never even seen it done. I was raised on a beef ranch."

"Beef cattle don't get milk fever," Dan said, "only dairy cattle, and heavy producers like these." He went into details on everything Dr. Andresen had done.

Hank Simmons stood, big hands thrust deep into his pockets, watching Dan and listening. "That was quite an experience," he said. "No wonder Frank says she's your calf. I'd say you had a big interest in Ginger, too."

They started back across the pasture to the barn and Beauty began dancing circles around Dan, small head lowered menacingly, tail up as she made threatening bleating sounds. Dan paid no attention to her and she slipped up behind him and belted him in the back. He whirled and ran at her swinging his arms, "Beat it," he yelled. "Go on. Scram!"

Beauty dashed off kicking up her heels and bleating as if she were frightened to death.

They went on to the barn and leaned against the building side by side. Simmons opened his coat, took off his hat, and dug his fingers through his mop of sandy hair. It was warm there with the late afternoon sun striking them. A small flock of starlings wheeled over the pasture and settled on the ground. A pair of gulls planed in from the river, circled a couple of times studying the ground, then flapped away toward the river again. Half the cows were lying down enjoying this winter warmth. Beauty was dancing around her mother again.

Hank Simmons swung a long arm toward the pasture and said, "Every time I see something like this I get the urge to go back to a ranch."

"Why don't you?" Dan asked.

"One of these days I will. Anyway, that's what I keep saying." Hank Simmons watched Beauty dancing around Ginger and observed, "That calf is going to make a fine addition to the herd."

"Mr. Edwards thinks she'll be a five-gallon cow."

"Hm-m-m."

"If she does," Dan said, "she'll furnish ten families with two quarts of milk every day."

"Hadn't thought of it that way. You ever figure how much the whole herd could furnish?"

"About one hundred and sixty families," Dan said promptly.

Hank Simmons looked impressed. "This farm's pretty important to a lot of people."

"It sure is. If we had a new barn and a milking parlor we could keep twice as many cows. We've got plenty of pasture to support them."

"Frank's been talking new barn for three years. How's the log salvaging coming?"

Dan shook his head. "We've gone almost a week without picking up a log."

"Then the barn'll have to wait another year. Too bad."

They talked a few minutes longer, then Hank Simmons glanced at his watch and straightened, "I could stand here and gab all day. I guess 'once a farmer always a farmer.' I'd better start moving or I won't get home tonight." He looked at Dan critically, "You're gaining weight."

"The way Mrs. Edwards cooks who wouldn't?" Dan said.

Hank Simmons felt of his arms. "It's not just beef. That's muscle." He punched Dan in the shoulder. "See you next trip. Tell Frank good-bye. And take good care of Beauty. Don't let what's her name, Blossom, get milk fever."

"I won't," Dan said, and watched Simmons stride up the hill to his car.

The car was running down the lane when Dan wondered if Hank Simmons had forgotten their agreement. He thought of their talk; all about Beauty, Ginger, Blossom, the need for a new barn, the log salvaging, how he'd helped Dr. Andresen. The big man had asked just the right questions, and had shown the proper amount of interest to get Dan talking. From what Dan had said he'd drawn his conclusions. He was pretty smart.

The boy stood there digging a toe into the soft earth and thinking about those conclusions. He heard the sounds about him and his mind automatically catalogued each. From the barn came the soft rasping of dry hay being forced through the trap door from the loft and falling with a whisper on the pile below. There was the rattle of Junior's chains. The pump started with a bang, then settled to a smooth hum. From the laying house came the industrious chatter of the hens.

What was it Mrs. Edwards had said that first night? "It's hard to hate things you understand and are interested in." His interest began the night Beauty was born, when a whole new world opened to him. But for her he'd have left here today bound for some unknown place where he'd start all over again. Then he'd never know if Beauty would make a good five-gallon cow, if Blossom would get milk fever, or if her calf would be as good as Beauty. He'd never know how the baby chicks turned out, how the salvaging was going, or if Mr. Edwards ever got that all-important new barn. If he hadn't happened to stay home that night, if Ginger hadn't become sick, and if he hadn't helped the vet he'd never have become all wrapped up in everything here. The difference had been so close it scared him. And all because of that little tan calf that was dancing around her mother and the gentle Blossom out there in the bright sunlight.

It didn't seem possible that he'd been here only a month. So much had happened and he'd changed in so many ways that he no longer felt like the same boy. For the first time in days he thought of the city, his home that was no home, the gang, the things they did, the streets they used to roam. It seemed to have happened to someone else a long time ago in another world. All those memories left him cold and he dismissed them from his mind. A lot of nothing, he told himself. What a waste!

Beauty had stopped dancing and was sedately following Ginger and Blossom who were moving leisurely toward the pasture gate. That inner clock, which all animals seem to possess, had told them it would soon be time to be let into the barn.

As Hank Simmons predicted, the rain held off for more than a week, and Dan put Beauty out in the pasture every day. Each morning when he turned her out of the maternity ward she had to have her romp. She'd dance stiff-legged circles around him, small head lowered as she made those menacing bleating sounds. All through this maneuver Dan kept turning to face her and talking to her. "You scare me," he'd say. "You really do. You look almost as fierce as Junior. But you're about as tough as a bowl of cream." She'd ram her head into his stomach and hold it there until he scratched under her chin and patted her neck. Then he'd put both hands against her forehead and shove. She'd promptly shove back, and for a minute they'd have a pushing contest with both of them slipping and sliding in the soft earth. Finally Dan would push her away or sidestep her lunge, and she'd rush around behind to bang him in the back.

Mr. Edwards took to standing in the barn door watching their morning tussle. "It won't be long before that's more than you can take," he observed when she slammed him particularly hard and sent him stumbling.

"It's almost more now," Dan panted and shoved her away. "Beat it! Go eat grass. I've got work to do." He ran at her flapping his arms. She raced away after the cows, bleating and kicking up her heels. Ginger and Blossom both stopped and waited for her.

The sunny weather came abruptly to an end one afternoon. They were booming back down the current, heading for home with two stray logs, when the black cloud boiled up over the distant mountains and began spreading down the valley with surprising speed. A gust of wind fled down the valley and ruffled the water. It came again, and again. Then it hit with a steady driving force that kicked up whitecaps and made *Methuselah* heel over. The boat began to pitch through the chop and Dan finally had to quit the bow for the protection of the wheelhouse. Nipper remained on deck, bracing his body against the drive of the wind, enjoying it.

"This old river can get nasty in a hurry," Mr. Edwards said peering out the window at the angry water. "Just possibly this could be winter's last gasp."

"How do you mean?" Dan asked.

"Spring's almost here. This could be the last storm of any consequence we'll get."

A few minutes later they pulled into the backwater, and for once Dan was glad to be off the river. The clouds were piling higher and higher, tumbling and churning with threat as they darkened the sky. They tied the logs to the stake line and made *Methuselah* fast, bow and stern, then went hurrying across the wind-swept pasture. The cattle, as if knowing a storm was coming, were bunched up at the gate leading to the barn. Dan noticed immediately that Beauty was not there.

"Probably down in the pasture somewhere," Mr. Edwards said. "But that's not unusual, especially with a storm brewing."

"I'm going to look." Dan turned back into the pasture. "Maybe she got hung up in the brush or something."

"That doesn't make sense," Mr. Edwards turned with him.

There were a number of brush patches scattered through the eighty-acre pasture and they searched them all, with Nipper ranging out ahead of them. "We can miss her if she's lying down somewhere or has been hurt," Mr. Edwards explained. "But Nipper will smell her out."

Dan ran and called Beauty's name and watched Nipper sniff carefully through the brush, tail waving, acting as if he knew what they were looking for. For the first time he felt a faint liking for the big black dog.

They covered the pasture but found no trace of Beauty. "Somehow she got through this five-strand barbed-wire fence," Mr. Edwards said. "It's never happened before. But that's what it's got to be."

"Why would she leave the other cows and Ginger?"

"Calves are like kids. Maybe she got to playing and

wandered too far and somehow got through the fence." Mr. Edwards scratched his head, "But which fence. Not the river side. She wouldn't try to swim the river. It's unlikely she'd get through the east fence. That's the newest and tightest. Let's try the south. We're close to it. Look for a loose lower strand or a barb with some calf hair sticking to it."

The wind struck a solid gust and Dan looked up. The black clouds now covered almost half the sky. A drop of wind-driven rain stung his face. "We'd better hurry," he said. "She'll get soaked."

"So will we," Mr. Edwards said. "Come on."

They searched the full length of the fence at a trot and found no loose wire, no barb with telltale hair sticking to it. They crawled through the fence and hiked into the open range beyond, with Nipper searching ahead of them. They could see for a mile and no living thing moved on the flat land.

"Nothing here," Mr. Edwards stopped. He called Nipper back. "Let's cross to the north fence. That's the last and our best bet. If you remember, the cows were feeding closest to that fence when we went to the river after lunch."

They recrossed the pasture at a trot, heads bent against the lash of the wind. Near them the barren brush was beginning to whip wildly and in the distance the river's surface was a mass of marching whitecaps. Fear began to build within Dan. Those black clouds had tumbled over them and were sweeping toward the lower end of the valley. Any minute they'd get it. The wind had a high-up dismal moan. It seemed he could smell the rain approaching. He panted, "Will this rain hurt her?"

Mr. Edwards shook his head, "Not likely. But it won't do her any good either. We want to find her as soon as possible."

"You've had calves get out before? You're still sure we'll find her?"

"Of course. Stock getting out is the oldest, most common plague a farmer knows. We'll find her. I'd just like to do it before the rain hits."

"Maybe she fell and broke a leg or—or something," Dan said fearfully.

"What's more likely is that she's wandered off too far and is lost. We'll find her hunched up under a bush to get out of the wind."

Mr. Edwards' confidence made Dan feel better.

They hit the north fence, turned and began following it, looking for a loose wire or hoof marks in the soft earth. Halfway down the fence they found a loose bottom strand with a few brown hairs stuck to a rusty barb. "This's where she went through," Mr. Edwards said. "She stretched this old wire a little. We'll find her off there."

In a few minutes they'd have her. Relief washed over Dan. He crawled through the fence and headed out across the uneven brushland. He bent forward against the steady smash of the wind. Nipper ran ahead again. A few big drops began to fall.

They progressed a good quarter of a mile searching every small ravine and brush patch. Fear began to mount in Dan again. Ahead lay even deeper ravines, great rock ledges, and a scattering of timber. If she had got in there she was going to be hard to find. The chances of falling into a steep ravine where she couldn't get out, or of breaking one of those spindly legs trying to climb over rock, were great.

Nipper suddenly let go with a burst of barking at the edge of a brush patch some fifty yards ahead. Dan shouted with relief, "Over here! Nipper's found her! We've found her!" and began to run. At first Dan could see nothing in the tall grass except Nipper's back and his tail sticking straight up as he stood there barking. He was about to yell at Mr. Edwards that Nipper had found something else when he saw the tan color. Then he saw her.

She lay on her side, small legs asprawl. Her neck was bent at a grotesque angle. Her chest was ripped open. He sank to his knees, and his hands touched her small head and stroked her smooth neck as he murmured brokenly over and over, "Beauty! Beauty! Oh, Beauty!"

Dan was aware that Mr. Edwards knelt beside him, that his big hands gently touched the gaping, bloody hole in her side. And he heard the man's voice, tender and infinitely sad, "Poor Beauty! Poor little beggar! She didn't have a chance. Heart's gone. So's the liver. Cougar, sure as the world. Came through this brush and jumped her. Broke her neck with the first swipe. She never knew what happened." Dan was vaguely aware that Nipper had moved off a few feet and was sniffing at the ground and growling in a manner he had never heard before.

This was Dan's first experience with violent death, and shock had torn through him leaving him numb. He was no longer conscious of the approaching storm, the cut of the wind. Beauty, who ran and played and joyfully kicked up her small heels in the winter sunshine, who rammed her head into his stomach and insisted upon a pushing battle every morning—his Beauty—was dead.

Dan couldn't stop stroking her neck and face. He didn't

want to look at the horribly torn, bloody side, but he couldn't help himself. A great lump came up in his throat. Tears stung his eyes. For a moment he was sick to his stomach. He swallowed hard and finally said in a harsh whisper, "We're going after him? We're going to kill him?"

Mr. Edwards shook his head. "That cat's long gone, Dan. I'd guess he was just passing through and stumbled across Beauty. Down here in the open amongst farms isn't cat country. How or why he came I can't even guess. But you can bet he won't stay around."

"Give me a gun," Dan choked. "I'll hunt him for a month. I'll never quit. I'll make him pay for this." He clenched his fists. "She was just a cute little calf having fun. She wasn't hurting anything."

"That's how it goes on a farm sometimes," Mr. Edwards said gently. "A farm means animals, and things can happen to them. They get lost. They get sick and sometimes die. They get hurt. Then again they're killed—like Beauty. A farmer learns to expect some losses. But you never get used to this sort of thing. You just try to protect against it."

"How do you protect against a cougar?"

"Keep your stock fenced. If this were cougar country we'd hunt him down and kill him. But it's not. He's probably miles from here by now and still traveling. We take our loss and go on."

"So he kills her and gets away with it!" Dan choked. He gently drew her small legs together and straightened her neck so that she lay as she had so often in life. A big drop fell and lay quivering on her cheek like a tear. Then the black sky opened and the rain came in wind-driven sheets.

five

They buried Beauty in the pasture where she had loved to run and kick up her heels in the bright winter sunshine. All through the chore Mr. Edwards remained grim and silent. When Doris Edwards learned of it she said with quick sympathy, "Oh, no! Poor Beauty. Can you do anything about the cougar?" Mr. Edwards shook his head, and she turned back to preparing supper, her lips pressed firmly together. Jennie promptly burst into tears and ran into her bedroom. When she finally reappeared her eyes were red and angry, her small chin was set.

"You're going after that cougar, aren't you, Pop?" she demanded. "You're going to kill him?"

"No," Mr. Edwards said and explained why they were not going to try to hunt down the cougar.

"Then I hope he meets a bear," Jennie said vengefully, "and gets clawed into a million pieces!"

The very next morning Dan caught himself going into the box stall to look for Beauty. Mr. Edwards saw the expression on the boy's face and said, "I did the same thing the first couple of times I lost a calf. It really hurt."

"It doesn't any more?"

"It always does. I've just learned to take it a little better now."

Unconsciously Dan kept looking for that small form dancing around Ginger and Blossom in the pasture. He kept expecting her to sneak up to belt him from behind.

The fiercest part of the storm had lasted a day and a half. Then it had slacked off, to be followed by intermittent clearing and a series of smaller storms that rolled down the valley, soaked the land for a few hours, and passed on.

Mr. Edwards and Dan fell into an easy pattern of work. Each knew what to do and they worked in companionable silence. Dan took his breaks to put grain in the mangers, gather eggs, and check on the baby chicks. The chicks were all feathered now. The brooder heat had been shut off and they were roosting. They were no longer considered baby chicks but young pullets.

Afternoons on the river never varied. Dan stood in the bow with Nipper and searched for logs while Mr. Edwards ran the boat. Dan had finally accepted Nipper's presence. He'd lost his fear of the big dog but he never petted him or made the slightest effort to attract the dog to him. Nipper constantly made friendly overtures which Dan ignored. He still didn't trust the dog. Their take of drifting logs was disappointingly few.

One night Mr. Edwards said, "I think it's time to put Blossom in the maternity ward. We're going to have to watch her awfully close for milk fever, too. I'll have to get up a couple of times a night to check her," he said thoughtfully. "Somehow these things seem to have a way of happening at night."

"What times will you be getting up?"

"About midnight, then again at three."

"How long do you think it will be before she calves?"

"When it gets this close it could be anytime. It should be in three days."

"Why don't we take turns checking her?" Dan asked. "You take the first night. I'll take the next." When Mr. Edwards said nothing Dan added, "I can tell if she's got milk fever and I can call you."

"I know you can tell," Mr. Edwards agreed. "I was just thinking that getting up at midnight, then again at three, is pretty hard on a growing boy. And you're growing at a good rate. It breaks up your sleep. You won't get much rest."

"It breaks up your sleep, too," Dan pointed out.

"All right," Mr. Edwards agreed. "I'll take the first night, you the second. We've got a spare alarm clock you can use on your nights."

Nothing happened on the first night, and Dan took the second. Mr. Edwards was right. It was hard getting up when the alarm shook him awake at midnight. He pulled on his clothes, stumbled down the stairs, got the flashlight from the kitchen table, and went out. Nipper rose from the porch and followed him down the hill to the barn.

Blossom lay in the deep straw of the maternity ward calmly chewing her cud. Dan went into the stall and talked to her and felt of her neck. There was no bow and she was warm. She made soft "m-m-m-m" sounds and licked his pants. He smiled and said, "You're okay," turned out the lights and ran back up the hill. He slipped out of his clothes, reset the alarm for 3:00 A.M. and fell into bed. Within minutes he was asleep.

It seemed he had barely gotten into bed when the alarm awoke him again and it was three o'clock.

Once more he crawled out of bed half asleep, dressed, and went down the stairs. This time Blossom was standing up eating hay and Dan didn't even bother going in. He returned to the house and fell into bed.

When Mr. Edwards awakened him at five thirty to milk, he felt he'd had no sleep at all.

Mr. Edwards checked her the third night and still there was nothing. Next morning he was a little concerned. "She seems to be healthy enough," he said as they stood leaning over the top rail looking in at her. "It'll be today, tonight, or sometime tomorrow," he predicted.

"Could anything else be wrong with her?" Dan asked.

"It's possible. But then she'd be sick and she's not." He straightened abruptly. "I always worry like an old mother hen with one chick when it's not necessary. Let's go."

Nothing happened during the day and Dan took the night again. He rolled out half asleep, dressed, went down the stairs, picked up the flashlight from the kitchen table, and went outside. It was becoming routine. Nipper rose and followed him down to the barn again.

Blossom was lying in the center of the stall, legs tucked under her. He remembered Ginger lying in the same position and went into the stall, felt of her neck and got her to turn her head. He looked at her eyes and they were clear. He looked at her a long minute, worried about something he could not name. Her breathing seemed a little heavy, but he was not sure. Anyway, there was no bow in her neck and her eyes were clear. She did not have milk fever—at least not yet. He'd be checking her in another three hours he told himself. There was nothing to worry about.

He returned to the house, fell into bed, and was promptly asleep.

Again the alarm woke him at three. He lay a minute savoring the blessedness of sleep. Then he felt himself drifting off and suddenly thought of Blossom. He sat bolt upright and swung his legs over the side of the bed. He dressed hurriedly, went downstairs, got the flashlight, and went out and down the hill.

Nipper jumped off the porch and trotted just ahead of him, leading the way.

Dan snapped on the barn lights and looked into the maternity ward. A great shock tore through him and suddenly he was wide awake. He scrubbed a hand frantically across his eyes, driving the last blur of sleep, and looked all about. Blossom was gone. The stall gate stood open. He knew instantly what had happened. In his half-asleep state at midnight he'd neglected to fasten the gate securely. She must be loose somewhere in the barn. He hurried down the line of resting cattle, crossed through the narrow aisle to the other section of the barn where the grain was kept. But she was not there. He spent minutes searching the lower barn but she was not there. Somehow she had got out of the barn.

He returned to the door leading to the pasture and

studied it carefully. It was not a large or heavy door. It was held closed by a small rope weighted by a piece of iron. The rope ran through a pulley and was fastened to a beam. He pushed it open with one finger. Then he noticed a handful of straw had wedged against the bottom of the door and held it open about four inches. He knew now what must have happened. When he had failed to lock her stall gate properly it had swung open. She had walked out, discovered this crack at the door, pushed her nose against it, and passed through into the dark pasture. But why would she leave the warm barn? To have her calf, of course. Cows always tried to get off by themselves. Tried to hide to give birth. It was a throwback to their wild days when they had to hide their young from roving predators. Blossom was somewhere out there in the eighty-acre pasture. She was giving birth, or already had her calf. Maybe she had milk fever now. All these terrible possibilities tumbled through Dan's mind as he ran out into the pasture.

It was very dark. The outline of a near brush patch was barely visible.

Dan threw the powerful beam of his flashlight into the nearest patch of brush and dived headlong into it. He cut the light right and left and found only brush. He thought of calling, but that would do no good. A cow never answered, besides she had come out here to find seclusion to have her calf. Brush slapped his face stinging and cutting, making his eyes water. It wrapped about his feet. He tripped and sprawled headlong. He searched through this one patch as best he could and burst out the far side. He stopped and swept the open pasture. The light beam picked up a traveling possum. It stopped and glared at him

95

with fiery eyes and lifted its lips in a snarl. Then it waddled unhurriedly off into the night. His eyes were becoming used to the dark. Fog banners ghosted across the land. The night breeze touched his face with the cold feel of rain. He plainly heard the far-off cry of a gull on the river.

It came to Dan how big this pasture was. He must search carefully through the dark to find her. This knowledge killed his first near rush of panic and he began to think calmly. In his mind he laid out the pasture in two halves. He would search this first half all the way to the river. If he didn't find Blossom he'd double back on the last half. That way he would cover it all and not miss any brush patches. He would most likely find Blossom in some brush patch, for in there she'd feel most hidden.

He moved forward again into the next brush patch searching more slowly, being careful as possible not to retrace his steps and miss any part of it. In this way he progressed all the way to the riverbank. He stood on the bank a moment looking at the dark, silent flow of water and thinking. Maybe she'd got through the fence as Beauty had and gone off into the brakes to have her calf. He dismissed that thought. It had been easy for small Beauty to get through that single lower strand of wire. It would be hard for a grown cow, and Blossom was no fence buster. She had to be somewhere in the pasture. He moved over to the farthest half of the pasture and began searching on his way back.

In a small, cleared spot in the very center of the first patch of brush he found her. The light beam caught her dead in its center. She stood facing him, ears pricked forward curiously, big eyes shining like diamonds. Dan lowered the beam and found the small, tan bundle curled at her feet. It was one big eye and a small head with spindly legs folded up against a shivering body. Dan's first thought was She's had the calf and she doesn't have milk fever.

He put his arms around Blossom's neck and patted her. She licked his pants and made soft sounds in her throat. "You had me scared," he told her. "You should have stayed in the barn where it was warm."

He bent to inspect the calf and was shocked. In the flashlight beam it was almost like looking at Beauty. It had the same small head, same color, the big liquid eyes. The calf was practically dry, which meant that Blossom had already cleaned it up. Then it must have been born more than an hour ago. He wondered if it had had its first drink of milk. He felt of Blossom's udder. It was tight and full. He doubted if the calf could get up alone yet. Dan laid the lit flashlight on the ground, got his hands under the calf, and lifted her up. She could not stand alone and he had to hold her. He boosted her into the proper position while Blossom waited patiently, turning her head to watch and making low "m-m-m" sounds in her throat.

The calf got the idea suddenly and began to suck noisily. Its tail switched back and forth sharply hitting Dan's legs. Dan began to smile. "You get a full belly," he told her, "then I'll carry you up to the barn."

When the calf began butting Blossom's udder, Dan pulled her away. He got the flashlight and stuffed it into his back pocket. He bent and put his arms around the calf's four legs and lifted. She was heavier than he'd thought.

Dan struggled across the small clearing with Blossom keeping close beside him. He had gone only a short distance when he stopped abruptly. His heart climbed into his throat and fear tore through him. Directly before him, not more than forty feet away, a pair of eyes glistened like live coals at the black edge of the encircling brush. There was no sound. He saw no body. But Dan knew immediately. Those unwavering eyes belonged to the cougar that had so brutally killed Beauty. The cat should be far up in the timbered mountains, but here it was, staring at him with the most deadly eyes he'd ever seen, planning ways to get at the calf in his arms.

It seemed to Dan he stood there a long time staring back at the cat's blazing eyes. Then his thoughts began racing. He had to get the calf out of his arms. He had to find some sort of weapon. He bent slowly and lowered the calf to the ground. He knelt beside it. His hand went out, searching through the grass for some sort of club, a broken limb,

The beam caught the whole cat in the pool of light.

anything. Then he remembered the flashlight. Wild animals were afraid of light. Dan eased the light stealthily from his pocket, aimed it at the pair of eyes, and pressed the button. The beam caught the whole cat in the pool of light. Dan saw the long, sleek body crouched close to the ground, the gleam of teeth as it spit, the lash of a long tail. Then it melted away. There was not a whisper of sound. Not a blade of grass or a bush moved. Just suddenly the cat was gone. He cut the beam about the clearing. There was nothing.

A low growl came at his elbow, and he whirled and flashed the light. Nipper stood beside him. The dog's eyes were fixed on the spot where the cat had been. His teeth were bared.

Impulsively Dan wrapped his arms around the dog's neck and drew him close. "Nipper!" he whispered, "oh, Nipper!

I'm so glad to see you. Stay with me, Nipper. Stay with me." Nipper twisted his big head and licked Dan's face. Then his eyes went to the brush again, and a growl rumbled deep in his chest.

Nipper had followed when he left the barn for the pasture. But because Dan had always avoided the dog, he must have stayed well behind. The dog's sudden appearance halted the rising fear which was threatening to panic the boy. Dan knelt on the ground beside the calf, held the dog close, and tried to think what he should do.

If Nipper would stay here and protect Blossom and her calf he could dash up to the house and wake Mr. Edwards. But the thought of entering that brush, even with the flashlight for protection, terrified him. And he didn't know if Nipper would stay, or if he could fight off the cougar if he did. The cougar had teeth as well as claws and he'd weigh fully as much as the dog. Blossom would be no help. She was terrified. She crowded close to Dan and the calf, big eyes searching, ears snapping back and forth to catch any sound. She would fight to protect her calf. But she was dehorned and therefore weaponless. All she could do was lower her head and butt. That was no defense against this powerful killer. Dan was afraid to try to carry the calf. He'd have to go through this very patch of brush where the cat lurked to get into the open, and he wouldn't be able to use the flashlight to help ward off the cougar. Even with Nipper to help him it was too dangerous. He thought of yelling at the top of his lungs. But the house was half a mile away and the Edwards' bedroom was on the opposite side of the house. Besides, yelling might infuriate the cougar into attacking.

Here, in the middle of this small opening was the safest place. The cougar would have to cross forty or fifty feet of open ground to get at them. Dan could hit him again with the light beam and the cougar did not like the light or the open. He had to stay here until daylight and until the cougar left, or until Mr. Edwards came out to milk, missed them, and began looking.

Then other worries began clawing at him. Would the cougar eventually become accustomed to the light? Was he so hungry that he might brave the light to get at the calf or the cow? How long would these batteries last? He seemed to remember he'd heard somewhere that they were good for seven hours. But these were not new batteries. There might be only an hour left. He looked into the east searching for the first faint bar of dawn. There was none. He wondered then what time it was. He had set the clock for three. It had taken a couple of minutes to dress. He'd spent maybe ten minutes looking for Blossom inside the barn. He'd been out in the pasture now maybe thirty minutes or a little more. It was still a couple of hours until daylight. He wondered how much help he could expect from Nipper. The dog's growl a minute ago had been brave enough. But was he just bluffing? A minute later Dan found out.

Dan caught the shine of eyes and flashed the light but he saw nothing. That instant Nipper let out a growl and tore out for the brush, barking at the top of his lungs. Dan kept the light on, flashing it around the open circle where he crouched. Then he shut it off. He heard Nipper crashing and barking a short distance off. After a couple of minutes there was silence. Then Nipper was back beside him again, tongue hanging out, panting. Dan patted him and said, "You did fine! Just fine. You and I are going to keep that old cougar away." Nipper lifted his nose and Dan felt the dog's warm tongue on his cheek. "I had you figured wrong all along," he said. "I'm sorry."

Nipper sat on his haunches beside Dan, ears forward, eyes searching the dark as if he knew what was expected of him.

Every few minutes Dan flashed the light around the little clearing but he did not see the cougar again. Then, just when he began to think the cougar might have left, Nipper growled and tore into the brush, barking. Dan followed him with the light until the dog disappeared. But he saw nothing and heard only the dog's angry barking. A few minutes later Nipper returned panting. Dan patted him and said, "You're doing a fine job. Good boy!"

He petted Blossom, too. The cow moved closer putting her head down every minute or so as though to reassure her calf and to lick it. The calf bleated several times and tried to rise but its legs were too weak.

Dan lifted it once, just after Nipper had again dashed into the brush growling and barking. He let the calf nurse for a good minute, then laid it down again. He kept searching the eastern horizon for that faint bar of light that would tell him daylight was coming.

A heavy mist drifted in and settled on the land. The flashlight beam could not cut through this sleazy mass to the brush. "It's up to you, Nipper," he said. "You've got to smell him out and keep him off us." The dog pricked up his ears and thumped his tail on the ground.

A cold rain began to fall. Dan turned the flashlight on

the calf and found it trembling. He peeled off his coat and spread it over the calf. Blossom lay down beside the calf and Dan pulled the calf close against her for warmth. Then he hunched down against the cow's back for what little protection he could find. Nipper sat beside him, head up, ever watchful. He didn't mind the rain.

In a few minutes Dan was soaked and the cold began to eat into him. His teeth commenced to chatter and his whole body shook. He wondered vaguely how long they'd been here. An hour, two hours? He wished he had a watch. He roused himself and flashed the light around a clearing that was turning soggy and was dripping with water.

His body became numb and his head sank forward on his chest. But for the constant rain he would have slept. He heard Nipper growl and go charging into the brush, barking. It was an effort to raise the flashlight and focus the beam. He was much too slow. Nipper had disappeared. He felt the calf under the coat. Its body was dry and warm and he smiled. Nipper returned and crouched down beside him again. Dan put a hand on the dog's wet coat and kept it there. "Good old Nipper," he murmured.

This was the way Mr. Edwards found them a short time later. "Dan," he said, "you're soaked to the bone! What happened?"

"Didn't close the gate right and she got out." His lips were stiff with cold. It was hard to talk.

"Why didn't you call me? There's no sense staying out here all night."

"Couldn't," Dan said. "When I found Blossom the cougar was here too."

"The cougar!"

"N-N-Nipper chased him away all night," Dan chattered. "I used the flashlight to help scare him."

"Well, he's gone now." Mr. Edwards took the coat from the calf and put it around Dan. "Beat it for the house. You're half frozen. I'll bring the calf."

"It'll get wet," Dan mumbled.

"Not much. Go on, Dan, get going."

Dan started to leave, then stopped and called, "Come on, Nipper, let's go home." The dog trotted up to him and the boy patted his head. Then boy and dog went off through the brush together.

Doris Edwards was getting breakfast when Dan walked in. Her eyes flew wide and she said, "Dan! What on earth? I thought you were milking. Why, you're soaking wet and you look like—like you've been up all night. Where have you been? What happened?"

Dan told her and she said, "The cougar! You've been holding him off all night. Good Lord! You run straight upstairs and get out of those clothes and rub yourself dry. Rub hard, mind, it'll get your circulation going again. When you've got on dry clothes come down and I'll have something hot for you to drink. Why, you could catch pneumonia. Hurry up."

Dan started up the stairs, then turned and asked, "Can Nipper come in? He's wet and cold, too. He was out there with me. I couldn't have done it alone."

Doris Edwards smiled. "I'll take care of Nipper. You go on."

It didn't take long to get out of his soaked clothes, towel himself vigorously, and put on dry clothing. It made him feel warmer on the surface but he still felt cold inside.

When he came downstairs Jennie was eating breakfast. In a corner Nipper was finishing a bowl of food.

Doris Edwards set a steaming cup of chocolate before Dan and said, "Get this inside you. It'll help warm you up."

Jennie said, "You do look cold. Your lips are all blue. Mom said you were out all night with Blossom and her calf, and that you and Nipper fought off that old cougar. What happened, Danny?"

"Leave Dan alone and eat your breakfast, Jennie," her mother said.

"But, Mom, I want to know. What's wrong with that?"

Dan picked up the cup of chocolate but his hand shook so he almost spilled it. He used both hands.

"You are cold!" Jennie said in a sympathetic voice.

Dan took a big swallow and felt the hot trail all the way to his stomach. Delicious warmth began to spread through him. He emptied half the cup before he put it down. He said to Jennie, "I left the gate to the maternity ward open and Blossom got out." Between swallows he told her about finding Blossom and how he and Nipper had kept the cougar at bay until Mr. Edwards came.

"Wow!" Jennie breathed, her brown eyes like saucers. "You sure were brave."

"Not me." Dan finished the last of the chocolate and Doris Edwards refilled the cup. "Nipper was."

Hearing his name Nipper came over and sat beside Dan. Dan patted his head and said, "You sure were."

"Did you see the cougar? Was he big?" Jennie asked.

"I saw him once for sure," Dan said. "He looked awful big to me."

"He might have got you," Jennie said in a hushed voice.

"Jennie," her mother said, "eat your breakfast and leave Dan alone."

"Well, he might!" Jennie insisted. "And how am I gonna learn things if I don't ask?"

"You can talk to Dan about it tonight when he feels more like talking. Can't you see he's worn out?"

"I'm sorry," Jennie said to Dan. "Don't forget tonight."

Dan nodded. He propped his elbow on the table and put his chin in his palm. In the warm room, with his stomach full of hot chocolate, he was getting sleepy.

Jennie asked softly, "What kind of a calf is it, Danny?"

"Heifer."

"Jennie . . ." her mother began.

"I'm all through. Honest, Mom. I just wanted to know that one thing." Jennie jumped up and began gathering her books together.

"Dan," Doris Edwards asked, "would you like something to eat now?"

"No," he said. In a minute he'd get up and go help with the milking. This warmth was like a drug. It went right through to his bones.

The kitchen door opened and Mr. Edwards came in. He asked, "You all right? Getting warm?"

"Yes," Dan said. "How's the calf?"

"The calf's fine. So's Blossom. You were right about that cougar. There's tracks all through the brush. He sure wanted that calf. It doesn't make sense him staying around down here. Maybe he's found killing calves easier than trying to run down deer."

Dan roused and asked, "What do we do about him now?"

"Hunt him down," Mr. Edwards' voice was tough. "We've got no choice."

"When?" Dan was coming awake again.

"Just as soon as you get some sleep," Mr. Edwards said grimly. "You go upstairs and hit the hay. I'll milk and clean the barn, then I'll go see Fred Hackett and borrow his rifle. We've got to get that cat or we stand to lose every calf that's born. You sleep till noon. You've got to be wide awake and sharp to hunt this fellow down."

Dan headed for the stairs. Behind him Jennie said excitedly, "Pop, can I go along?"

"And miss school?" Mr. Edwards asked.

"Just today. Only one day, Pop. Please."

"You're going to school," Mr. Edwards said. "This is a job. We're not doing it for fun."

"He killed Beauty," Jennie said darkly. "He deserves to die."

"Maybe he does." Doris Edwards' voice was sharp. "But you stop that kind of talk. Understand?"

Dan climbed the stairs, closed the door and fell on the bed, clothes and all. He pulled a cover over him. Jennie was right. He felt the same way about the cougar. But a small fear chased through him as he remembered those wicked eyes staring at him through the dark, the shape of the long slinky body melting into the brush without a sound, without the movement of a twig or a blade of grass.

six

Dan slept until noon and then the faint aroma of food cooking drifted up the stairway and shook him awake. Half asleep he lay there for a minute listening to the sounds of movement from downstairs. Then he remembered the cougar and sat bolt upright. He climbed out of bed, dressed quickly, and went downstairs.

The table was set and Doris Edwards was hurrying about, putting lunch out for them. Mr. Edwards sat in a kitchen chair holding the biggest, most deadly looking rifle Dan had ever seen. A second and smaller rifle lay on a chair near him.

Doris Edwards asked, "How did you sleep?"

"I feel like I died I slept so hard."

"Good. Do you think you might be getting a cold or anything?"

"No," Dan said. "I feel fine." He looked at Mr. Edwards and asked, "How's Blossom and the calf?"

"Great! You should see that little beggar eat." Mr. Edwards hefted the rifle, then abruptly brought it to his shoulder and sighted at something through the window.

Dan asked, "Are we going after the cougar this afternoon?"

"Just as soon as we have lunch." He indicated the rifle he held. "I borrowed it from Fred Hackett this morning so we'd each have a gun. That's yours on the chair. Have you ever handled a rifle, Dan?"

Dan shook his head. "I've never handled any kind of gun."

"As soon as we finish eating we'll head out and you can do a little practicing before we start to hunt in earnest. You'll use this smaller rifle of mine. It's big enough to kill any animal in North America. You'll find it easier and lighter to handle than this cannon of Fred's."

Doris Edwards said, "Put the rifle down, Frank. Lunch is ready."

While they ate, Dan asked, "Is the barn work all done?"

"No, and Doris helped, too. She put the grain in the mangers, took care of the pullets, and gathered the eggs for me. I got the barn cleaned but I didn't get the hay down. We'll have to do that when we come back from hunting."

Doris Edwards asked, "Where are you two going to hunt?"

"Off in those brakes where we found Beauty."

"You be careful," she cautioned.

"From what I understand they don't often attack people unless there's a shortage of deer and rabbits and such small game."

"Then his food supply must be running short," Doris Edwards pointed out. "Which means he could attack you."

"We'll be careful," Mr. Edwards smiled.

When they left the house Dan carried the light rifle and had a pocketful of shells. Nipper jumped off the porch and trotted up to Dan, tail waving. Dan patted his head and asked, "Did you have a good sleep, too?" Nipper lifted his lips in a grin and trotted down the hill ahead of them.

They stopped at the barn to look in on Blossom and her calf. The calf was a small tan bundle curled up in the straw. It was almost like looking at Beauty except that this calf had a white spot about the size of a dollar in the center of its forehead. "Can I take care of this one and raise her, like I was doing with Beauty?" Dan asked.

"That's a good idea," Mr. Edwards said. "You were doing a fine job with Beauty. . . . Well, let's go."

They left the barn and started across the pasture. The morning's rain had stopped, but the sky was low and gray. The ground underfoot was soggy.

Nipper trotted in front of them and began casting back and forth. Dan called, "Don't you get too far ahead and maybe scare that cougar."

Nipper looked back and showed his teeth in a grin, then stopped and waited for them. Dan patted the dog's head and Nipper grabbed his hand in his big jaws and shook it, growling playfully.

Mr. Edwards said, "I was beginning to wonder if you two would ever hit it off."

"It wasn't his fault we didn't. He tried to be friends. If it hadn't been for him last night, I don't know what I'd have done."

Halfway across the pasture they stopped and Mr. Edwards said, "Let's load up here. Your gun holds six shells, one in the barrel and five in the magazine. It loads here. Put in five, pump one into the barrel, add the extra one to the magazine and press this little button, your safety, from right to left. Be sure it's on at all times. Take it off only when you're about to shoot. When you're through, put it on immediately. All right, load up."

Dan loaded the rifle and put the safety on.

"Now you're ready to kill a cougar," Mr. Edwards said.

"I've never fired a rifle, or any kind of gun," Dan said. "Maybe I can't hit anything."

"Let's go down to the river and find out."

They sat side by side on the riverbank and Mr. Edwards explained, "The back sight is called a peep sight. I think you'll find it easier to handle than the scope I've got on this big one. Get your eye up close to that little round disk and look through the pinhole in the center. Now you can see the front sight."

"I can see the whole river," Dan said surprised.

"That's right. Now notice that little round ball on top of the front sight. Put that ball on whatever you want to hit and pull the trigger. That's all there is to it. All right, stretch out on the ground on your stomach, prop up your elbows and pick something floating to shoot at."

Dan flopped on his stomach, got the rifle in position, and studied the moving water for a target. Suddenly his hands were wet and his mouth dry.

Mr. Edwards was saying, "Remember, don't jerk the trigger. Squeeze off the shot so you don't move the rifle muzzle. Jiggle the muzzle a hundredth of an inch and you can miss by five feet." He pointed, "There's a floating stick. Try that. And take your time. Don't pull until you're on target."

The stick, about two feet long and several inches wide, swept smoothly along in the current. The tiny knob on the front sight almost covered the width of the stick. Dan tried to hold on the center of the stick, and he was suddenly conscious of his heart hammering against his ribs. His breathing made the sight wobble. He held his breath and concentrated on the stick and the small knob on the sight. When he thought he had it he began to squeeze the trigger. He wasn't ready for the thundering explosion. The stock slammed back against his shoulder almost numbing it. A fountain of water shot into the air several feet beyond the stick.

"You shot high," Mr. Edwards said. "Pump out the empty and try again. Take plenty of time. Hold the butt tight to your shoulder and the kick won't hurt."

The second shot was six inches under.

"You've got time for another before it floats out of sight," Mr. Edwards said.

The stick was little more than a floating line on the water now. This shot was high but Dan guessed it had gone over the stick by no more than an inch or two.

Mr. Edwards nodded, "You're getting the feel of it. There'll be another target along soon. Each time try to remember just where you held on the target, that way you can correct on the next shot."

A minute later a small, round piece of limb floated by. "Try that," Mr. Edwards said.

Dan knew just what to expect of the rifle now. He drew down on the limb and was on it almost immediately. He squeezed off. The stick exploded into two pieces.

"Good boy!" Mr. Edwards said. "You've got two shells left. Try for the pieces."

The first piece Dan hit and broke again. The last shot missed but was so close the stick jumped completely out of the water.

"That's plenty good enough," Mr. Edwards said. "Any one of those last shots would have killed a cougar. Load up again. Let's get moving."

Dan stuffed shells into the rifle and asked, "Would it have killed a cougar that far away?"

"Eight or ten times farther. In fact, as far as you can see him you can kill if you hit him right. But hit him any place to stop him or slow him up. Now there's a couple of ways you can carry a rifle when you're looking for game and may want to shoot quick. One is in the crook of your arm, like this, provided you're sure the muzzle isn't pointed at someone. The other is in both hands with the stock snugged up under your armpit so you can swing it straight up fast, the muzzle pointing straight ahead and down. I'll be on your left, so carry yours pointing ahead and down. Don't shoot in my direction at all and I won't in yours."

They recrossed the pasture heading for the north fence, with Nipper trotting back and forth close in front of them.

Dan glanced at Mr. Edwards. He carried the big rifle slung in the crook of his arm. His face was set, his long, square jaw was stubborn. Dan thought of the rifles, then of the cougar. He pictured those fiery eyes watching him, the long, slinking body crouched close to the ground. He remembered how the cougar had spit at him with hate and anger, ears laid flat, open mouth exposing gleaming teeth. A knot of cold dread settled in the pit of Dan's stomach.

They crawled through the north fence and headed into the rough land. They passed the spot where Beauty had been attacked and killed. Dan looked at the spot and remembered. The dread left, and he was filled with determination to hunt down and kill the cougar.

Mr. Edwards stopped and said, "This is the country where we'll find him. It's rough and rocky, some timber and brush, good hiding places for a cougar. We'll separate a couple of hundred feet and make a sweep straight ahead for a mile or so. Move slowly and carefully and above all be quiet. Keep your eyes open for high places where he might be lying, like a tree limb, a rock, or a high mound. They like to get up where they can look over the country and spot for game. Watch the ground for signs that he's been around, such as a half-eaten rabbit or other animal he might have killed. I can see Nipper's going with you from now on. He's your dog now, so don't let him get too far ahead. Keep him up close or he might jump the cat and scare him clear out of the country before we can get a shot or even see him. And be mighty careful you're aiming at the cougar and not your dog. It's better not to get a shot at all than to kill Nipper. If you see anything suspicious sing out. All right. Here we go."

Dan called Nipper to him. They moved off a short distance to the right. Mr. Edwards went an equal distance to the left. Then they turned and began to move across the rough land, walking slowly. Mr. Edwards carried his rifle across his chest where he could swing it fast in any direction. Dan carried his with the muzzle pointed at the ground. He knew he could swing it up fast. Nipper moved before him, nosing through grass and brush and sniffing around rocks. Dan called him back softly when the dog got too far out front. "You stay close," he patted the big head. "Stay close, Nipper. Stay." Soon Nipper seemed to understand and strayed only a few feet ahead.

Dan kept a sharp lookout but he saw nothing. It was very still. He could not hear Mr. Edwards several hundred feet away. Dan glimpsed him at intervals, moving slowly, looking all about, rifle ready for instant use. A killdeer exploded out of the grass at Dan's feet startling him. It ran ahead dragging one wing and calling piteously, "Dee-dee-dee." He glanced down and found its crude nest of sticks with three speckled eggs almost under his feet. He stepped carefully over it and went on. A hawk sailed soundlessly over the brush ahead, dipping in and out, so close Dan could see its cold eyes searching the grass for mice or ground squirrels or any smaller unwary bird. A pair of crows began scolding from a treetop. They kept it up until the hunters had passed.

They went on and on across the rugged land and found no sign of the cougar. Finally Mr. Edwards drifted toward Dan and they stopped and sat on a rock to rest. Nipper flopped on the ground panting.

"It'll happen every time," Mr. Edwards grumbled. "You never see a thing when you've got a gun. We'll rest a few minutes then take a big swing to the left and start back."

"Do you suppose he has left this time for good?" Dan asked.

"No telling." Mr. Edwards squinted up at the distant rimrock. "He could be holed up somewhere up there sleeping off a big meal. He could just as easy be fifteen or twenty miles away killing some other farmer's calf. They do a lot of traveling."

They hunted the remainder of the afternoon, wandering back and forth across the rugged country. They found nothing. Finally Mr. Edwards said, "We've got to quit. It's almost time to milk and we've still got to knock down hay for tonight." They returned across the pasture and the cows were waiting at the barn to get in.

They unloaded the rifles, spent a half hour getting down hay, then let the cows in.

After they finished milking they went to the house. Jennie was just finishing setting the table. She asked immediately, "Did you get the cougar?"

"No," Mr. Edwards said.

Jennie was disappointed. "I thought you'd have his hide nailed solid to the barn tonight."

Doris Edwards shook her head, "What a way to express it!"

"That's what the kids say," Jennie said. "What's wrong with it?"

"Well, nothing really, I suppose."

"What your mother's trying to say is that it's not necessary to sound quite so bloodthirsty," Mr. Edwards said.

"But, Pop, you want him dead. Don't you?"

"Of course."

"Well?" Jennie spread her hands as if that settled the matter and went on setting the table.

Dan and Mr. Edwards stood the rifles in a corner and Doris Edwards asked, "No sign of him?"

"Not a thing."

"Will you try again tomorrow?"

"We have to."

"Maybe this time he's gone for good. Maybe Dan and Nipper scared him off."

"Dan had the same thought. We're going to try to make sure."

They were eating dinner when Jennie asked suddenly, "Has anybody named Blossom's calf?"

"No," Mr. Edwards said, "got any ideas?"

"How about calling her Beauty, too?"

Dan said, "I'd rather have some other name."

Doris Edwards glanced at Dan and said, "So would I. There was only one Beauty."

"How about Brownie? Or Spot, for that white spot in the middle of her forehead?" Mr. Edwards asked.

Doris Edwards wrinkled her nose and shook her head, "I think she's awfully cute. How about Dolly?"

"We could call her Trixie because that was a mean trick her mother pulled on Dan last night," Jennie said. "How about Trixie?"

"Maybe we ought to call her Scaredy." Dan smiled. "That's what we all were down there in that brush patch."

"Is that where you found her?" Doris Edwards asked.

"Right in the middle of a patch of vine maple and wild rose bushes," Mr. Edwards said.

"That's it!" Doris Edwards said. "That's what we'll call her."

"Scaredy?" Jennie asked. "Aw, Mom."

"No, silly. Rosie."

"Rosie?" Mr. Edwards thought about it, then nodded. "Not bad. Blossom's baby. Sort of symbolic, too."

"Okay by me," Jennie said.

"Dan?" Mr. Edwards asked.

"Fine with me."

So Blossom's offspring was named.

Dan and Mr. Edwards hunted for two more days, searching carefully for any faint trace that would lead them to the cat. They looked for a paw print in soft earth where he might have gone to drink, the remains of animals that he'd eaten. Up around the rimrocks they hunted among narrow crevices and rocky caves for stray cat hair or bones of prey or any other sign of a big animal having been about. They found nothing. The third evening they waited until dark then slipped down into the pasture to the brushy spot where Blossom had given birth. There they crouched in the brush for several hours hoping the cougar might return.

When they finally quit for the night Mr. Edwards said, "He's either not around or he's too smart for us. I don't see much use hunting any more. But there's one other thing I'm going to do before I call it quits. Tomorrow afternoon we contact every other ranch in this area and see if anyone has lost stock, or seen a cougar or any sign of one."

Dan went along with him and they visited a half a dozen ranches. No one had lost stock or seen a cougar. "That settles it," Mr. Edwards said as they drove toward home. "I'll bet he's left the country. We might as well call this hunting off. I'll take Fred Hackett's rifle back. Tomorrow we start looking for logs again."

"Suppose he's still around?" Dan asked. "We'll be turning Rosie out in the pasture soon."

"We've hunted three days for him," Mr. Edwards pointed out, "we've visited every ranch in the area and there isn't a sign that he's around. We can't go on looking, without some sort of a lead."

"I don't want to lose Rosie."

"Neither do I. But you can't hunt a thing that doesn't seem to exist. We've got other work to do. And we need every stray log we can pick up for that new barn. I guess you'd call this a calculated risk, but we have to take it."

Jennie complained bitterly. "I wanted you to kill him. Are you sure he's gone, Pop?"

"Sure as we can be."

"I'm satisfied," Doris Edwards said. "Just so he's gone."

With the cougar hunting out of the way Dan gave more care and attention to weaning Rosie. He did not break her of nursing as fast as he had Beauty but Mr. Edwards said it had been done in good time. She developed the same trick of pushing her head into Dan's stomach and wanting to play. Dan played with her just as he had with Beauty. And like Beauty, she would belt him from behind whenever the opportunity came. As the days passed and he continued to care for Rosie, he discovered the sharp memory of Beauty was fading. When he thought of her, the hurt was only a dull ache. He spoke of this to Mr. Edwards.

"Sure you feel bad. So do I. But we can't let the loss of one throw us when we've got so many more to care for. That's the way it should be."

"I'm sort of scared to let her out in the pasture," Dan said. "Aren't you?"

"Yes," Mr. Edwards agreed. "But almost two weeks have gone by and we've looked coming and going to the river every day and haven't found a trace of that cat. We've got to assume he's left for other parts. But we'll keep watching. That's the only precaution we can take."

On the few sunny days they began turning Rosie out into the pasture with the herd. When they returned from the river late each afternoon, Dan looked anxiously for her. He didn't realize Mr. Edwards was doing the same until he didn't see her one day. Mr. Edwards suddenly said, "There she is, between Blossom and Ginger. Looks like Ginger is assuming part of the care of Rosie, now that she doesn't have Beauty."

Rosie had been out in the pasture a half dozen times before Dan's fears finally subsided.

The river was creeping up. Dan could see the added swiftness of the current. When they took *Methuselah* out now for their daily log hunting he felt the current grab at her with a giant's strength. He tinkered often with the old motor to be sure it stayed in top condition to buck the added strength of the river. The only time Dan touched the wheel was when he worked on *Methuselah* alone in the backwater. Then he would sometimes start the motor, ease it into gear, and move the boat just the short distance ahead and back that took up the slack in the mooring lines.

"This high, swift water will bounce some big ones out of the rafts soon," Mr. Edwards predicted. "We've got to keep a sharp eye out now. Those babies are worth real money."

Two days later they caught a really big log. It was a cold, drizzly day with a sharp wind that kicked up whitecaps and made the river particularly rough. They were some three miles upriver and were coming home empty. The old motor was turning over smoothly. *Methuselah* dipped into the troughs, spewed water over the bow drenching Dan and Nipper, and rolled over the crests. Wind slapped Dan's slicker against his body and drove fine rain into his face like needles. Dan and Nipper spotted the log at the same moment. It was rolling like a whale in the rough water ahead of them. Nipper began to bark and dance. Dan swung an arm and pointed. Mr. Edwards nodded, advanced the throttle, and they bore down upon the log.

It was the biggest log Dan had seen floating free. It was about forty feet long and at least four feet through. Maneuvering close enough to catch it in this choppy current without smashing the boat's stern proved a delicate job. Again and again they drew near but the log was rolling and pitching so hard Mr. Edwards was afraid to close in. It was a good twenty minutes before they got the job done.

Mr. Edwards clapped Dan on the back and grinned, "That's a log that is a log! It'll be worth three times as much as those runts we've been catching. Now let's go home."

They were plowing down the river with the log in tow when Dan and Nipper spotted another log opposite Arrowhead Island. Nipper began barking and dancing again. Dan pointed. Mr. Edwards opened the throttle and ran for it. He called out the window, "That one will really make this 'a day's pay for a day's work.' "

Dan watched the log and gauged their speed. It was

going to be close. In another five minutes the log would be sucked into the current of Suicide Run and lost to them.

Mr. Edwards cut straight down the river and overhauled the log swiftly. Then he turned up-current to meet it. They caught it just short of the Run. It was less than half the size of the big one they now had. But it was well worth catching.

Dan slammed the pike pole into the end and led it aft. Nipper went wild again. He barked at the top of his lungs. He dashed madly about the deck, through one door of the wheelhouse and out the other. Then he leaned over the stern and kept barking furiously at the log.

Mr. Edwards cut the motor and ran aft with the sledge hammer and six-foot length of chain to secure the log to the boat. Dan held the log close with the pike pole and Mr. Edwards leaned over the stern to drive the spike into the top of the log.

Methuselah's stern rose and fell in the rough water. The log rolled and bobbed in spite of all Dan's efforts to hold it still. Mr. Edwards had to time his hammer swings perfectly when log and stern rose together. The first two swings set the spike. He raised the hammer for a final smash to drive the spike home. The stern and log rose together and the hammer went down. That moment the nose of the log fell into a trough and Dan could not hold it. The stern of the boat continued to rise. The sledge missed cleanly and the momentum of the heavy hammer pulled the man off balance. He pitched overboard into the river and disappeared.

A moment later Mr. Edwards surfaced some twenty feet away. He had lost his sou'wester and his black hair was pasted to his forehead. Dan wrenched the pike pole out of the log, leaned over the stern, and reached toward him with it. He was a bare four feet short.

Mr. Edwards tried to swim toward the pike pole but the long raincoat hampered his arms. He sank again. It was an eternity before his dark head bobbed to the surface. He was farther away than ever. He had managed to shed the raincoat and he tried to swim toward the boat. He was downriver from Dan and no matter how hard he stroked the powerful current carried him farther away. Nipper leaned over the stern and began to bark at the struggling man.

Dan rushed into the wheelhouse to throw the motor in gear and ease up beside Mr. Edwards where he could reach him with the pike pole. The motor had died. He pressed the starter frantically. The starter hummed but the motor did not catch. He pressed it again and again with no results. Nipper, sensing trouble, kept barking at Mr. Edwards.

Dan tried the starter again and searched the three gauges to see if they would tell him anything. They did not. The boat surged suddenly forward and he glanced up. They had passed the point of Arrowhead Island and were caught in the murderous current of Suicide Run. Ahead of him Mr. Edwards was being tossed about and was fighting to keep his head above water. Another minute or two in this millrace with all those clothes on he'd be sucked under for good. Dan pressed the starter again. He could not understand why a motor he'd worked so hard on, that had been running so smoothly, wouldn't start. Then he glanced back and saw the trouble.

The distributor cap was knocked sideways. Nipper, in his

mad dashing back and forth when they'd caught the last log, had struck the cap and broken it loose. Dan rushed to the motor, snapped off the cap and glanced at it. The rotor was broken. No electricity was getting through. The motor would never start with this broken rotor.

Dan remembered the old loose rotor he'd replaced the first time he worked on the motor. He'd tossed that rotor into the toolbox. If it wasn't broken . . . He dug into the toolbox and found the rotor at the bottom under a pair of heavy wrenches. It was not broken. He jerked off the damaged rotor, pressed the old one in place and replaced the distributor cap. Then, holding his breath, he pressed the starter again.

There was no telling what would happen with an old worn-out rotor that had lain in the grease of a toolbox for months. The starter hummed. Dan eased out the choke and tried again. The motor caught for a single explosion. Dan kept his finger on the starter, eased the choke out full, then closed it. Suddenly the motor roared to life. Dan yanked the throttle wide, put the motor in gear and spun the wheel. *Methuselah* came around, motor roaring, and headed downstream rolling and pitching, spray exploding from her bow.

Dan searched the tumbling water for Mr. Edwards. He was nowhere in sight. Suddenly Nipper began to dance and bark. A hundred feet ahead Mr. Edwards' head bobbed for an instant at the top of a wave then slid into the trough and was lost. Dan kept watching the spot. The man's head rose out of the trough and Nipper barked frantically. They were closer now and Dan could see the exhaustion on the man's face, the tired way his arms flailed out.

Dan passed within forty feet of him at full throttle. He dared not stop going downstream. The log he was towing would smash into the stern of the boat and sink it. He had to get below Mr. Edwards and turn upstream so the current would keep the log pulling away from the boat and he'd have control.

When Dan made his turn he found he could not come in close to Mr. Edwards. The swift current had slammed the man against a huge rock and he was clinging to its slippery surface by some small crevice Dan couldn't see. But he'd never be able to hang on more than a minute or two. That clawing current would rip him loose. Dan edged *Methuselah* as close as he dared and shouted out the pilothouse window. "Let go! I'll catch you. Let go! Let go!"

Mr. Edwards turned his head, and Dan could see him gauging his chances. Then his fingers loosened and the current tumbled him toward Dan.

Dan held the throttle open just enough to keep headway and waited. When the man was almost upon him he cut the motor, kicked it out of gear so the boat would drift, grabbed the pike pole and thrust it out. Mr. Edwards grabbed it, and Dan pulled him to the side of the boat.

Mr. Edwards was too exhausted to help himself much, and it took all Dan's strength to pull him up and roll him over the side. Dan left him lying on the deck and rushed back inside, slammed the motor in gear, and yanked the throttle wide. *Methuselah*'s old motor roared and the scarred bow dug into the savage current. Inch by inch she fought her way back upstream out of the deadly grip of Suicide Run.

Mr. Edwards stumbled into the wheelhouse and collapsed on a box. He bent over holding his sides, gagging and choking and spitting up water.

They finally rounded the point of Arrowhead Island and were again in the main channel where the current was not so strong. Dan cut the motor back until they hung motionless in the water and turned to Mr. Edwards, "You all right?"

"I think I damaged some ribs when I hit that rock. They hurt something fierce." His voice was little more than an exhausted whisper. "When I got into Suicide Run I thought sure I was a goner." He glanced out the door and said, "I see you even saved our log."

"I'd have cut it loose but I didn't dare take the time."

"What happened?" Mr. Edwards managed. "I could see you working in here. Did the motor die?"

"Nipper hit the distributor cap when he dashed through here and knocked it loose. The spinning rotor hit the side of the cap and broke. I found the old rotor I'd taken out several months ago in the bottom of the toolbox and put it in. Luckily it still worked."

Mr. Edwards shook his head in wonderment and muttered, "Oh, good Lord! Good Lord!"

Dan asked, "You feel good enough to take the wheel now?"

Mr. Edwards looked up then, his long face drawn and pale with pain and exhaustion. He managed a very small smile and whispered, "Why don't you just take us home, Skipper?"

seven

When Dan got Mr. Edwards up to the house and explained what had happened, Doris Edwards said, "We're going to the doctor right now. Broken or cracked ribs are nothing to fool around with. We shouldn't be gone more than a couple of hours, Dan."

"If you're not back in time I'll let in the cows and start the milking," Dan said.

They returned within two hours and Mr. Edwards explained ruefully, "Three cracked ribs. They've got me all taped up. Can't do any heavy work for maybe three, four weeks."

Jennie asked sympathetically, "Does it hurt bad, Pop?"

"Not when I stand all humped over this way. If I could just stand straight. If I could just take a deep breath."

"Danny's gonna have to do all the heavy work now."

Mr. Edwards nodded and looked at Dan soberly, "I sure hate to saddle you with all this."

"We'll make out," Dan said. "You can be the boss, but I'd better start setting my alarm clock again."

So Dan took over the heavy work. Mr. Edwards watched him cleaning the barn alone the second day and grumbled, "Now I'm putting the grain in the mangers, checking the pullets, and gathering the eggs. Funny how things turn out sometimes."

"I just wish I could do this faster," Dan said. "I'm so slow it's cutting our time down on the river something fierce."

"You're doing it fast enough. Maybe we're not losing as much on the river as we'd like to think. Anyway, the real spring high water hasn't come yet. That's when we'll snag the most logs. I'll be good as new by then."

But it worried Dan. No matter how hard he worked it was always late afternoon before they made their slow way to the river. And some days they didn't make it at all. Mr. Edwards still handled the boat. "Hanging on to that wheel is about all I'm good for now," he confessed. "If you can manage the pike pole and the chain and sledge hammer, we're still in business. But for the love of Mike don't do a stupid thing like I did and fall overboard."

So they continued their search on the river but their catches remained too few. "If I could just get enough for that new barn," Mr. Edwards said, "I wouldn't care if I never saw a log again."

It was the first week after Mr. Edwards' accident that Hank Simmons returned. They had come in from a late run on the river, and Mr. Edwards made his slow way up to the house to rest. Dan let in the cattle and was in the maternity ward having a pushing match with Rosie when Simmons walked in. He wrinkled up his nose and sniffed, "What's that smell I'm getting? Could it be cows?"

"You don't really remember?" Dan asked, and shoved Rosie away.

Simmons leaned on the stall, long arms and big hands dangling over the top rail. "I sort of seem to remember it from when I was about your age." He stretched out a long arm. "How's it going, Dan?"

"Fine." Dan looked at his hand lost in Simmons' huge paw. "Did you ever play football?" he asked.

"Three years in college. I played end; snagged a few pretty fair passes in that time."

"I'll bet you did. Did you play pro ball?"

"I wanted to. I had a couple of good offers. But the Doc said No. I'd picked up a bad knee. If I got busted there again, they said I'd likely be a cripple for life. That's no good for a guy that's going back to a farm someday." He looked closely at Rosie and asked, "Isn't this a new one? As I seem to remember the other one, what was her name, Beauty, didn't have a white spot on her forehead and she was bigger."

"This is Rosie, Blossom's calf." He scratched Rosie's ears. "Beauty was killed by a cougar about a week after you were here."

"Oh, no!" Simmons' voice was full of sympathy. "Tell me about it."

Dan told him and Simmons shook his head, "That's tough. Did you get the cougar?"

"We didn't hunt him right then. Mr. Edwards thought he was just passing through as this isn't cougar country. But when Rosie was born the cougar tried to get her." He told Simmons about it and added, "After that we hunted him for three days and never even found a sign."

"Those cats cover a lot of territory," Simmons said. "He may never be back. But you'd better keep your eyes peeled." He glanced about the barn. "Where's Frank?"

"Up at the house resting."

"Resting!"

Dan told him about the accident on the river and Simmons shook his head, "Things have really been happening since I was here last. You got any more hair-raising experiences to tell me?" And when Dan said No, "Then I guess I'd better look in on Frank."

They walked up the hill to the house together. Hank Simmons was silent, scowling down at his feet. Just before they reached the house he said, "I saw your uncle and talked with his doctor."

"How's he doing?" Then at the odd look on Simmons' face he stopped and asked, "Is anything wrong with Uncle Harry?"

"No, he's better. But it'll be a long time before he gets out of that place." He rubbed his face thoughtfully. "How much did you think of your uncle, Dan?"

Dan thought about that odd question. Then he said, "I lived with him for five years. He wasn't home much, especially the last year or so. I guess I liked him all right. He was my uncle. He's all the family I've got."

"Do you want to go back to him?"

"I hadn't thought much about it lately," Dan confessed. He did now. He thought about leaving the farm, and Mr. Edwards and Doris Edwards and Jennie. He thought of not going out on the river again, of never seeing Blossom or Rosie or even that ugly old Junior. He compared this life with the one he'd led with his uncle. A dingy house where he was alone most of the time. "No," he said, "I don't want to go back," and he felt a small sense of guilt at saying it. "Are you trying to tell me something?"

Simmons nodded. "I've been trying to find some easy way for two days. Now I guess I don't have to, so I'll just say it. I had quite a long talk with your uncle the other day. And like I said, he is better. But he's not out of the woods yet. I brought up this business about you coming back to him at the end of the year, and he told me he didn't want the responsibility of caring for a boy again."

"He never cared for me. I did that myself."

"I gathered as much. But that's how he feels about it."

"What happens when my year's up here?"

"As long as he doesn't want you, you'll still be a ward of the court for a couple of years."

"You mean, I go to another home?"

"Or stay here. Why don't I talk to Frank and Doris about it?"

Dan considered. He'd like to stay here. But what about the Edwards family? They'd agreed to take him for one year. Once they got the new barn Mr. Edwards would be able to manage the farm very well alone. If they knew about his uncle they'd probably offer to keep him. They might feel they had to. Dan didn't want that.

Simmons asked, "Anything bothering you?"

Dan nodded. "I'd like to stay here more than anything. You know that. But I can't."

"Why not?"

Dan kicked at a rock and muttered, "They might think they had to keep me."

"Had to? Oh! you mean because of the way you helped the vet save Beauty that time and catching Frank in the river last week?"

"Yes."

"I see." Simmons bit his lip thoughtfully. "It does put you in an awkward position," he agreed. "But if you leave here they'll need another man to take your place. Ever thought of that?"

"They won't. I've seen pictures of the kind of barn Mr. Edwards is planning. All automatic. Automatic watering, feeding, a milking parlor where six cows come in at a time, are milked, then turned out, and six more come in. All the things we do by hand now will be push button. He'll be able to take care of more than twice as many cows alone as we're doing together. That means he'll be able to cut out one man and save money. I know that's what he plans. That's the whole object of the new barn. If they agreed to keep me after that they'd just be making a place for me. I don't want to be any—any—"

"Freeloader?" Hank Simmons asked quietly.

"That's right."

Simmons studied the boy soberly for a minute then said, "You're getting to be quite a man."

"It's true, isn't it?"

"If everything is like you say, yes. Why don't we just let

this lie for now? You've still got about eight months here."

"All right," Dan agreed.

Mr. Edwards called from the kitchen door, "Hey, you two! Come in here out of the rain to do your powwowing."

He shook hands with Simmons and asked, "Anything wrong?"

"No," Simmons said.

"You two looked serious enough to be settling all the troubles in the world," Mr. Edwards said.

"Dan was telling me how you got a couple of cracked ribs. Went for a swim in the middle of the winter, and with all your clothes on. You should know better."

"I should, at that," Mr. Edwards agreed. "He lifted me right out of the middle of Suicide Run about as slick as a fisherman netting a salmon."

"Suicide Run!" Hank Simmons glanced at Dan. "He just said he helped you back aboard."

Doris Edwards put a steaming cup of coffee on the table for Hank Simmons and said, "Frank would have drowned but for Dan. Dan even had to repair the motor before he could rescue Frank."

Simmons sipped his coffee and said, "Maybe somebody else better tell me just what happened. And start at the beginning. It seems our friend here left out some of the most important parts."

Doris Edwards told him the whole story, her brown eyes big with apprehension, and even Dan thought it sounded pretty dramatic.

Hank Simmons sipped his coffee and listened, glancing at Dan from time to time. When she'd finished he said to Mr. Edwards, "You were one lucky guy. Only other man I ever knew to come out of there was Joe Benjamin. He got caught in old Suicide and his boat was smashed. He hung on to a plank and rode it all the way through. He was more dead than alive when they fished him out."

"So was I," Mr. Edwards said.

Hank Simmons finished his coffee and rose. "I've got to be getting back. See you later. And, Frank, no more winter swims."

Simmons was almost to the door when Mr. Edwards asked, "Seen Dan's uncle lately?"

"Yes, about a week ago."

"I believe you said he was in the State Hospital." Mr. Edwards smoothed the tablecloth and added idly, "I didn't know you were covering the hospitals, too."

"I'm not. I was just curious to see how he was doing."

"And how's that?"

"Well, he's not a young man," Simmons hedged. "His doctor says he's as good as can be expected."

"Pretty slow," Mr. Edwards said.

Outside, standing beside the car, Simmons said to Dan, "You were right. They'd keep you now no matter what it cost them. They feel a tremendous sense of gratitude to you, and they should. You did save Frank's life." Simmons punched his shoulder. "Don't worry about it, Dan. We'll cross that bridge when we get to it. A lot can happen in eight months."

"Sure," Dan said and watched Simmons get in his car and drive away.

The rain slacked off and they had several days during which the sun shone part of the time. They let Rosie into the pasture with the cows. Dan still did the heavy work around the barn, and now Nipper was forever at his heels.

"Looks like you've got a dog, whether you want him or not," Mr. Edwards observed.

"I'll take him." Dan patted the dog's head and Nipper grabbed his hand in his mouth and worried it, pretending to growl.

Mr. Edwards insisted his ribs felt better but he still could not handle a pitchfork or lift anything heavy. When they went to the river he walked slowly and had to stop to catch his breath. "It's this darn tape," he explained. "It's so tight it shuts off my breath. I can't straighten up."

A light, steady rain set in again, and Dan left Rosie complaining loudly in the maternity ward. Afterward he was sure that single act saved her life.

They were returning from the river and Mr. Edwards walked slowly, bent over. "Certainly wasn't much of a day. That scrawny toothpick we got will just about pay the gas bill."

"Yes." Dan was only half listening. Nipper was exploring ahead of them, tail waving. Several hundred yards beyond him the cows were bunched, heads turned, staring toward a brush patch. Nipper trotted toward the brush. Suddenly he stopped, his tail stiffened, his body grew tense. Dan saw all this, and then he saw something else—a long, tawny body faded silently into the brush without disturbing a single limb. The next instant Nipper lunged forward barking furiously. Dan yelled and pointed.

"The cougar! The cougar!"

Nipper dived headlong into the brush and disappeared. The next instant the cougar burst out the far side running in long, graceful bounds, its tail streaming straight out behind. Nipper followed, running his hardest, big body low to the ground, barking at the top of his lungs.

Cougar and dog streaked across the open pasture. The cat was making toward the north fence and the rough, tree-studded country beyond.

"That cat won't stay on the ground long with Nipper so close to his tail," Mr. Edwards said. "He'll tree. Run to the house and get the rifle. I'll follow them as fast as I can. Nipper and I can keep the cat treed until you get back."

Dan dashed past the frightened cows, across the pasture, through the barnyard and up the hill to the house.

Doris Edwards turned from the stove when he burst into the kitchen with a startled, "Good heavens, Dan! What's wrong?"

"Cougar!" Dan panted and dived into the closet for the rifle and handful of shells.

"You be careful. Mind!" Doris Edwards called after him as he sprinted back down the hill.

Dan raced across the pasture with the rifle in one hand, the shells in the other. Halfway across he could hear Nipper barking. Then he glimpsed Mr. Edwards ahead of him. He had just crawled through the north fence and was half running, half walking, bent over holding his side. A second later the brush swallowed him. Dan heard the man's voice added to Nipper's barking. The cougar must have treed.

Then the fierce exertion of running claimed all his thoughts. He was tiring. His legs began to ache. His lungs were on fire. Pain stabbed through his chest as he reached for more air. But still the ground flew beneath his feet. He reached the fence, dived through, and ran on.

He burst out of a small patch of brush and there, in a cleared spot under a single fir tree were Nipper and Mr. Edwards. Nipper was looking up the tree, fairly dancing with excitement. Mr. Edwards held a piece of broken limb. Every few seconds he added his voice to Nipper's. Then he'd bend over holding his sides.

Dan skidded to a stop and began stuffing shells into the rifle while he looked up the tree. About forty feet above the ground the cougar stood in the crotch of a big limb. He resembled a giant house cat and his yellow eyes looked down straight into Dan's. His long tail snapped back and forth angrily. His lips lifted in a snarl exposing gleaming fangs. Dan pumped a shell into the barrel and handed the rifle to Mr. Edwards.

Mr. Edwards pushed the gun away. "Can't straighten up enough to shoot, can't get my breath," he panted. "You take him."

"I can't." Dan was in sudden panic. "I've never killed anything. I might miss."

"You hit a drifting stick a lot smaller and three times as far away. This is just another stick, only it's stationary and a lot closer. Come on, boy, get at it. This is the cat that killed Beauty and almost got Rosie. He's not going to stay up there all day."

Dan stepped back and looked up at the cougar. He drew a deep breath, raised the rifle and brought his eye close to the deep sight. Through the tiny hole he saw the whole cougar. He could feel his heart hammering and the labored pumping of his lungs.

Mr. Edwards' voice said calmly, "Take plenty of time. Aim for just below the ear."

Dan was surprised at how quickly he came on target. This was much easier than shooting at a small bobbing stick in the river. He held his breath, laid the little knob on the front sight an inch beneath the cougar's ear and began squeezing the trigger. The sharp explosion startled him. He felt the backward kick of the rifle and through the peep sight he saw the great cat come tumbling out of the tree. It struck the ground with a solid thud and was still. Nipper rushed in, grabbed the cat by the neck and worried it, growling fiercely. When the cat did not respond the dog stopped and just stood there looking at the dead animal.

Dan and Mr. Edwards moved forward cautiously and knelt beside the cougar. Dan reached out almost fearfully and touched the soft fur. Mr. Edwards said, "Right below the ear. A good shot. Well, that's the end of our trouble with him."

Dan was amazed. A minute ago there had been such electric excitement and racket. With the simple crooking of his finger it was gone and the great cat lay here before him completely harmless. This was the cougar that had killed Beauty, that had glared at him from the dark, and held him prisoner all night in a brush patch. The cat they had hunted for three days and found not a trace of. Had he been carefully hidden all this time, or had he returned from some great distance to kill another calf? They'd never know.

"Take plenty of time. Aim for just below the ear."

The slow fall of the fine rain glistened like silver on the cat's coat. Beside Dan, Nipper sat. Off somewhere a startled killdeer made a noisy "dee-dee-dee" and was answered. A pair of small brown birds flitted through the bare branches nearby, then suddenly fled with faint sounds of alarm.

Dan stroked the cat's body. He felt its warmth and the dampness of its fur. He remembered the beautiful, silent way it could move and he could no longer hate it. He was glad their troubles were over and that Rosie and the other calves to come would be safe. But he was sorry for the cat, too. His emotions were all mixed up.

Mr. Edwards said, "See if you can find a piece of loose wire along the fence so we can tie his feet together. I'll look for a pole to string him on. We'll carry him up to the barn and skin him out."

They had the cougar partially skinned out on the barn floor when Jennie and Doris Edwards came in. Doris Edwards said, "My, he is a big fellow. What a beautiful hide!" Then she just stood there and watched.

Jennie walked all around the cat her brown eyes wide. "Wow!" she breathed. "Look at those claws, and those teeth! I'll bet he could tear your head right off with those teeth!" She squatted beside them and asked, "What're you going to do with the hide, Pop?"

"Send it in with the milk truck in the morning. They'll drop it off at the tannery and they can make a rug of it for us."

"Where'll you put the rug?"

"In Dan's room. It's his cougar. He killed it."

"You killed him, Danny? No fooling?" Jennie's eyes were big and shining. "How many times did you shoot him?"

"Once." Dan showed her the bullet hole.

"Gee!" Jennie said admiringly, "you sure clobbered him good. Didn't he, Mom?"

"Jennie!" Doris Edwards said, annoyed. "This was a job Dan and your father had to do. Can't you get that through your head?"

"Can I ever! Just wait till old Comb-His-Hair Eddie hears about this," Jennie crowed.

eight

The rain tapered off and they could turn Rosie out into the pasture again with no worry.

The subject of Hank Simmons' last visit remained uppermost in Dan's mind. The dread of leaving here was a dull ache that never left. It was with him every minute as he worked in the barn. It rode with him on the river. It went to bed with him at night and was the first thought in his mind in the morning. The new barn became the symbol of his staying or leaving. Every log they found brought Mr. Edwards closer to the new barn and made his own departure more sure. With each log he was happy for the Edwards family and sorry for himself. Things are sure crazy, he thought. Nothing makes sense.

He tried to think of ways he could make himself indispensable. Mr. Edwards was no mechanic. There was the tractor, but it was fairly new and these modern machines went thousands of hours with very little repair. The boat *Methuselah?* Mr. Edwards had said that once he got the new barn he didn't care if he never saw another log. That would end the need for *Methuselah*. There was a mowing machine, also a side-delivery rake for haying. Both were simple machines and neither used a motor. And they were needed just a few days once a year. The new push-button barn would have all electric motors and Dan's ability was with gas engines. He might as well face it. There was no place for him here under any circumstances.

He was thinking about this one morning leaning on the pitchfork when Mr. Edwards asked, "Anything wrong, Dan?"

"No," the boy shook his head. "I was just—just thinking."

A week had passed when Mr. Edwards announced one morning that he was going in to the doctor to have the tape removed from his chest.

"You're sure your ribs are healed?" Doris Edwards asked anxiously. "You've had no pain or anything?"

"Why should I? Dan's been doing all the work. It's about time I started doing my share. Everything feels all right. But I can't tell with all this tape. I want it off so I can make sure." He left right after breakfast saying, "I might be a little late. I've got to stop by the co-op office, too."

Mr. Edwards was late. Dan was half through the milking and was feeding Rosie in the maternity ward when he came

143

in. "Tape's gone," he announced. "Everything's fine. Now you can take it a little easier."

The next afternoon when they went aboard *Methuselah*, Mr. Edwards took the pike pole and went into the bow with Nipper. "All right," he said to Dan, "let's get going."

That week two important things happened. The tanned cougar rug was returned and spread on the floor in Dan's room, and Hank Simmons returned. They had let the cows into the barn early because it was raining. Dan was standing at the head of the line watching them eating, when a big hand dropped on his shoulder and Simmons' voice asked, "How goes the battle?"

"Fine," Dan said.

"Ever see the cougar again?"

"He's a rug on the floor of my room."

"You killed him?"

Dan told the big man all about treeing the cougar and killing him. Simmons thumbed his hat onto the back of his head and grinned. "Man! I'd like to have been in on that. Son of a gun! You sure have things happening around here." He asked again, "Everything okay?"

"Sure," Dan said. "What brings you out here so soon?"

Simmons didn't answer. He looked around and asked, "Frank's ribs get all right?"

"They're fine now."

Mr. Edwards came down the line of cows from Junior's stall and shook hands with Simmons. "I was wondering how soon you'd get here."

"I got your message," Simmons said. "I came as soon as I could. What's up, Frank?"

"Let's go up to the house," Mr. Edwards said. "Come on, Dan."

"I could start milking," Dan said.

"It's early yet. You'd better come up to the house, too."

Dan glanced at Hank Simmons. Simmons shrugged and they followed Mr. Edwards out of the barn and up the hill.

Simmons said, "Dan tells me you got the cougar."

"Not me. Dan shot him."

Simmons scowled at Dan. "You're always leaving out the most important part of the stories. Cut it out!"

Doris Edwards said, "Why, Hank, what're you doing here?"

"You don't know?" Simmons asked her.

"Know what?" she asked.

Mr. Edwards said, "Why don't we all sit down."

"Frank, what is this?" Doris Edwards demanded.

"Sit down, Doris," Mr. Edwards said. "Dan, Hank, pull up chairs."

They sat down around the kitchen table and all looked at Mr. Edwards. Doris Edwards said, "Frank's been up to something. I can always tell. He's got that smug, sly look."

Mr. Edwards just smiled and spoke directly to Hank Simmons. "The last time you were here you and Dan stood out there in the rain and talked for a good five minutes. I could tell it was pretty serious talk. Ever since then Dan's had something heavy on his mind. I remembered that when you left that day I'd asked you about Dan's uncle. You'd told me before that he was in the hospital. Well, you didn't give me a straight-out answer. That's not like

145

you. In all the years I've known you, you never evaded a direct answer before. I began wondering and I started putting things together. When I went in to have this tape taken off my ribs, I ran up to the State Hospital and saw Dan's uncle. I had a long talk with his doctor, too."

"That's why you were so late," Doris Edwards accused. "You didn't stop at the co-op office at all. Why, you big fraud."

"That's me," Mr. Edwards agreed.

Doris Edwards glanced around at the other faces and said, "Apparently I'm the only one here who doesn't know what's going on. Will someone tell me?"

Mr. Edwards said, "If Dan's uncle ever gets out of the hospital, and his doctor has some doubts, he doesn't want to assume custody of Dan any more."

"What?" Doris Edwards demanded, shocked.

"Isn't that right?" Mr. Edwards asked Hank Simmons. "That's what you and Dan were talking about in the rain that day. That's what has been bothering Dan ever since; where he'll go when his year is up and he leaves here. Isn't that right, Dan?"

Dan looked at Hank Simmons then at Mr. Edwards, "Yes," he said.

"Frank, why didn't you tell me?" Doris Edwards demanded.

"You'd just have got upset. I looked into it when I went to town. I left word at Hank's office to come see us. I've got an idea. I wanted him here when we talked things over. You and Dan might want to ask him some questions." He looked at Dan. "Are you satisfied here with us? I mean do you like it?"

"Yes," Dan said. "But I think you know that."

Mr. Edwards nodded. "I wanted to hear you say it." He turned to his wife, his gray eyes direct, his long face sober. "I've been thinking for some time I'd like to make this arrangement permanent. What do you say?"

Doris Edwards looked from Dan to Hank Simmons then back at her husband. Color flooded into her cheeks. Suddenly she smiled, her eyes shining. Impulsively she reached across the table for his hand, "Oh, Frank, I think it's wonderful! Simply wonderful!" Her voice was soft and husky. "It's what I've wanted from the very beginning."

Mr. Edwards looked at Simmons. "How about it, Hank? Can we do it?"

"Just a minute." Simmons laid his big hands flat on the table. His face was a study of surprise and disbelief. "Let's get this straight." His eyes went from one to the other of them. "You say you want to make this permanent. Is that right?"

"That's right." Mr. Edwards nodded vigorously.

"You know exactly what that means? Both of you know?"

"Well of course." Doris Edwards laughed happily. "What's wrong with you, Hank?"

"You throw something like this at me out of a clear sky and then ask what's wrong?" Simmons said. "I'll tell you what's wrong. I need time to think what all this involves."

"Well—take time—but start working on it," Mr. Edwards smiled.

"You're sure? You're both dead sure?" Simmons looked at each of them.

Both of them nodded. "We're sure."

Hank Simmons smiled at Dan. "How about that? I guess it's up to you now. Do you know what we're talking about, Dan?"

"I—I think so. About me living here."

"More than that. They said permanently. They'd like to adopt you. That means you'd be a regular member of the family the same as Jennie."

"You'd change your name, too, to Edwards. What do you say?" Mr. Edwards asked.

A great surge of elation rushed through Dan, and was as suddenly gone. Of course he knew why they were doing this, and the dull ache was back again, only this time much worse.

Hank Simmons was watching him closely. He said, "Dan, tell them what's bothering you." When Dan looked at him surprised, "Go on, tell them exactly what you told me that night we stood outside in the rain."

Dan looked at Mr. and Mrs. Edwards. He drew a deep breath as if it might be his last and said directly to Mr. Edwards, "I've been reading some of those farm magazines, all about the kind of new barn you want and everything. Once you get that barn you won't need me. Not even to take care of twice as many cows. You'll even have extra time to do other things that you don't have now because you won't be catching logs on the river anymore. You're doing this just because of what happened on the river and that night Beauty was born. I don't want it that way. I want . . . I want . . ." He shook his head and bogged down completely.

Hank Simmons helped him out, "Dan's trying to say that he doesn't want to trade on any feeling of obligation."

"Why, that's not true!" Doris Edwards said quickly. "We really want you. Remember that first night up in your room when I told you I wanted this to work, Dan? Well, this is what I meant."

"Maybe," Dan said miserably, "but this other hadn't happened that night."

"It doesn't make a bit of difference."

"Just a minute," Mr. Edwards said. "Dan's right. Of course it makes a difference. Everything he's said is true."

"Frank!" Doris Edwards said in a shocked voice.

"Hold it." Mr. Edwards held up a hand and kept looking at Dan. "We haven't worked together every day these past months without getting to know each other pretty well. Certainly he knows we have a feeling of obligation to him. And he knows that it's bound to color any decision we make. He's been reading about those new push-button barns and he's right there, too." He spoke directly to Dan then and said, "We've never talked about all the changes a new barn will bring because there didn't seem to be any reason to. Now there is. I'm going to lay it all out to you exactly as I've planned it. Then you tell me if you think it's still a one-man job.

"Now then, we've got a hundred-and-eighty acres here. So far we're using only a little over eighty, that includes all the outbuildings and the pasture. That leaves roughly a hundred yet to develop. That right?"

"Yes," Dan said.

"With the new barn I'd like to more than double our cows. I'd like to go to about sixty. I could still handle that alone. But there won't be enough pasture for that many, without irrigation in the summer to keep the grass growing.

We'll have to irrigate. We'll break up the eighty-acre pasture into about five plots with cross fences. While the cattle feed on one we'll irrigate the others. We'll move the cattle from plot to plot as fast as they eat the grass down. Those sprinkler pipes should be moved every eight hours and some of that piping will be almost half a mile long. It takes three to four hours for one man to make a move. Now the new barn will also have two big silos. Here's where we'll begin to use that hundred acres. We'll put in about forty acres of corn to fill our own silos. That corn has to be cultivated and irrigated regularly. The sixty acres that's left we'll put into alfalfa for our own hay. That alfalfa has to be irrigated, too. In the fall we've got to harvest the corn and fill the silos with it, harvest the alfalfa, and fill the barn. Now, do you think one man can do all that?"

"No, sir." Dan was smiling. "Never. I didn't know about all those things."

"Then one last thing. You should know by now that we not only need you, we want you. Satisfied?"

"You bet I'm satisfied."

"All right," Simmons said, "we're back to the first question. How do you feel about this adoption, Dan, about changing your name, becoming a full-fledged member of this family?"

Dan thought about changing his name. He said it over in his mind several times, Dan Edwards. Dan Edwards. He liked the sound. He smiled at Doris and Mr. Edwards. He spread his hands and said, "It's swell. I think it's just swell."

The door burst open and Jennie breezed in from school.

She thumped her books on the drainboard and tossed a general "Hi" into the room. Then she stopped and looked at them. "Is anything wrong?" she asked. "Everybody's so serious."

Doris pulled out a chair and said, "Sit down, Jennie. We've got something to tell you."

Jennie sat down, her brown eyes going from face to face. "Why's everybody sitting around making like a tragedy?"

"If you'll be quiet for one minute I'll tell you."

"Okay." Jennie folded her hands in her lap. "I'm quiet."

Her mother explained about the adoption and when she'd finished Jennie's brown eyes were dancing. "Does that mean Danny'll be a sort of a brother?"

"That's right," Mr. Edwards said.

"Wow! that's neat!" Jennie jumped up. "That's real cool! It just goes to show; if you want something long enough you'll get it."

"What's that, Jennie?" Simmons asked.

"A brother. I've been wanting one since the day I was born." She nibbled a finger thoughtfully and asked, "You'll be going to school next fall, won't you, Danny?"

"Of course," Mr. Edwards said.

"We'll both be in second year high," Jennie followed her thought. "We'll be having the same classes. You can help me with my math."

"You'll do your own math," her mother said.

"Heck," Jennie grumbled. "Doing school work together is part of the fun of having a brother," she said, and flounced from the room.

"I guess that's it," Hank Simmons said, "unless you've got something else on your mind, Frank."

Mr. Edwards shook his head. "What happens now?"

"I'll bring the papers out for you to sign in a couple of days. After that you'll all be on probation for a year. I'll make regular reports. If, at any time during the year any one of you, Dan or Doris or Frank, wants to call this whole thing off, all you have to do is say that you don't want to go through with it. At the end of the year if all of you are still of the same mind, you'll appear before the judge and he'll make it final. Now, does everyone understand that?"

Jennie popped back into the kitchen. "How about me? Suppose I'm not satisfied?"

"Hold it, Jennie!" Mr. Edwards said.

"But, Pop, Mr. Simmons said everybody."

"If you're not satisfied, Jennie, we'll give it careful consideration," Simmons said.

"Okay," Jennie smiled at Dan. "Don't worry, I'll be satisfied. I just want to be included." With that she disappeared back into the living room.

"That Jennie . . ." Doris Edwards shook her head.

"Well, I'll be getting back." Simmons rose and stood smiling down at Dan. "You asked me once why I didn't go back to the farm. This is one of the reasons. Once in a while a situation works out like this. Then I feel my work's really worthwhile." He ruffled Dan's brown hair with a big hand. "See you in a couple of days."

After Simmons had left, the three people still sat at the table. Doris Edwards smiled, her eyes very bright. "Well, Dan," she said, "well!" She drew a deep breath.

Dan nodded. He couldn't say a word.

Mr. Edwards finally said, "Getting a little late. Maybe we'd better get at the milking."

Dan couldn't sleep that night for thinking about the day's happenings. He thought of his uncle, the home, the gang he'd hung out with and the streets they'd roamed. He waited for that special feeling of loss, of loneliness. It was not there. This was home now. This was real.

Three days later Hank Simmons returned with the necessary papers. Mr. Edwards and Doris Edwards read them and signed where Hank Simmons indicated. "That's it," the big man said folding the papers. "Now we go for a year. And don't forget, at the end of that time you all still have to want this. Any of you can stop it, right up to the minute you stand before the judge. Well, I've got to go. Frank, spring is well along."

"Yes, I noticed," Mr. Edwards agreed.

In the city Dan had never been particularly conscious of the coming of spring. Here he was. He noticed the green sheen that had replaced the dull brown of bare limbs on the brush patches. On close inspection he found the limbs covered with green buds bursting into leaf. The heads of grass clumps began to rise up. The first green spears appeared. The cows, and particularly Rosie who was just beginning to eat grass, searched out these tender shoots and snipped them off. A flock of geese went over, heading north, so high he could not see them and only the sound filtered down. He saw them for the first time on the river. A great flock had settled to rest on the sand of Arrowhead Island. Flights of ducks went over, flying low and fast and straight. Dan could see their eyes and hear the whisper of wings. "They'll go two or three thousand miles," Mr. Edwards said. "They'll nest in the land of the long night and the midnight sun. This fall they'll all fly back accompanied by their young."

Crossing the pasture with Nipper one day Dan suddenly realized the half-green brush patches were a mass of moving yellow. Thousands of tiny canaries were darting about through the brush feeding on partially opened buds. Abruptly the flock took off in a yellow cloud that swerved and swooped across the land. Robins followed the canaries, hopping about the pasture putting on tugs of war with huge angleworms. Dan heard his first meadow lark. It was sitting on a fence post pouring its heart into song. He watched it spring into the air and climb straight up, singing all the way. The wind funneled down the valley, soft to his cheek. The rain lost its biting edge. They left Rosie out, even in the rain now, and she ran and kicked up her small heels. For this was spring.

One day as they were making ready for their run on the river Dan noticed the water was up a foot. The next day it was up another foot and he spoke of it to Mr. Edwards. "I know," the man said, "we need this warm rain to stop completely and the weather to turn cool for a while so that big snowpack in the mountains will melt more slowly. Then the river can handle it."

"We're in for trouble. The Columbia is one of the world's greatest rivers, Dan. It's more than 1200 miles long and drains over a quarter of a million square miles of land, including part of the Rocky Mountains. It has eight times as much water flow as the Colorado River and almost double that of the Nile. I've seen this old river climb into flood almost overnight. Then it's pretty ugly. We don't want that."

Day and night the soft rain continued. It was pushed down the valley by a warm spring wind that sliced deep into the heaviest snowpack in years. The river rose steadily. Its current increased and its surface roughened. The water turned from clear blue to coffee brown. Dan tinkered with *Methuselah*'s motor almost every day. She had to stay in top condition to buck this current.

The number of floating logs increased. Now there were some big ones. Not a day went by that they did not return with two or three, and sometimes they had in tow all *Methuselah* could handle. "It's the high water," Mr. Edwards explained. "The higher it gets the more logs will bounce out of the rafts."

Logs began piling up in the backwater. It was not long before they had assembled a small raft. Mr. Edwards said happily, "Barring some kind of accident our chances of getting that new barn are beginning to look awfully good." Then he looked at the gauge he had nailed to a piling and frowned. "River's up another two feet. I don't like that."

Every night they turned on the radio and listened to the latest news. Now the airways were filled with flood talk. The river was eight feet above flood stage. Sauvies Island, at the lower edge of Portland, was under water for the first time in years. The houses on the island had been flooded. The families had been evacuated. The seriousness of it did not come to Dan until he saw a picture in the morning paper of men sandbagging the sea wall as water poured over the top. Another showed a man rowing a boat down Portland's Third Street.

That night the call went out over the radio for men to man miles of dikes along low banks inside the city limits.

Waterfront industries were flooded out. An oceangoing freighter had been torn loose from her moorings and swirled downstream for two miles in the grip of the flood before it finally came to rest against a mudbank. Thousands of acres of lower valley farms and orchards were under water. People and livestock had fled to higher land. Roads leading into the city were flooded and traffic had to be rerouted. Trains could not reach Union Station. A picture in the paper showed a man holding a three-foot-long fish he'd caught swimming in the lobby of the Union Station.

And day after day the soft rain fell and the warm wind blew.

The river was dotted with floating stumps, trees, a floating dock, a walkway with the railing still intact. The roof of a small building went by with a drenched rooster perched miserably on the ridge. The river spilled over the bank and lapped at the foot of the pasture.

Dan had to be particularly watchful now that a tree or stump or some other floating debris didn't crash into *Methuselah* and sink her. They were catching logs like mad. Every trip they came into the backwater towing all the old motor could handle. They filled the backwater with logs, and Mr. Edwards predicted they'd sell them for more than enough to build the new barn. "If only we don't lose 'em," he said. "This water could get so high they'd break loose and float away." Against that danger they stretched another hundred feet of cable to reinforce the existing one. The earth had absorbed all the water it could. The pasture now stood several inches deep in rain water. This moved in a solid sheet across the pasture to the river.

One morning Jennie started for school and a half hour

later returned. "Bus can't get through," she announced. "Road's washed out."

That night the radio mentioned the upriver dike for the first time. They were in the middle of supper and listening to the news. The announcer said, "Sixty miles upriver a five-mile stretch of dike that holds the river in its channel across low land is in danger of going out. The water is within inches of the top. If this dike goes the whole valley right down to the city will be flooded. Thousands of head of livestock could be lost. A half dozen small towns hugging the riverbank would be flooded. Lives could be lost. Damage to property would run into millions. The governor has authorized the use of prisoners from the State Prison Honor Farm. Eight truckloads of men have been rushed to the dike. They will sandbag the dike to hold back the river."

Jennie's eyes were big. "Do you think we'll have a flood, Pop?"

Doris Edwards asked in a frightened voice, "Frank, what are we going to do?"

"We're going to sit right here," Mr. Edwards said calmly. "You've heard that kind of scare talk before. You know how these newscasters always build up a story so it sounds big."

"But they never sandbagged the dike before."

"That doesn't mean the dike's going out," Mr. Edwards explained. "Sandbagging is done to protect it so they'll be sure it won't go out. It's not a new thing. They've been sandbagging some of our biggest rivers almost yearly for almost a century. It's a precautionary measure. I'd rather they did it and told us about it, than not do it and say nothing. Relax. We're going to stay right here and we'll be all right."

No one found much interest in eating after that and they kept the radio on all evening. News came every hour and everyone, even Mr. Edwards, stopped whatever he was doing to listen. The same news item about the dike was repeated each hour but, Dan noticed, nothing new was added. He began to relax.

"But prisoners," Doris Edwards said.

"Why not?" Mr. Edwards said. "They'll use only husky fellows. That's what it takes to handle bags of sand hour after hour."

Dan kept thinking of the prisoners filling sandbags and fighting the rising river. The picture he built in his mind of them, rushing about filling bags of sand and building a wall to hold the river back, fascinated him.

Next day when they started out upon the river in *Methuselah*, Dan asked, "How far is it up to the dike where the prisoners are working?"

"Eight, maybe nine miles."

"Is that too far for us to go? I'd sure like to see what they're doing."

"Just piling a string of sandbags on top of the dike to hold back the water," Mr. Edwards said.

"I suppose so."

"But you'd like to see it?"

"Yes, I would."

"I guess I would, too, at your age. Okay, you're the skipper."

It took more than an hour to run up there because they were bucking a strong current. Dan ran close to shore to avoid most of the debris. Today they didn't pass one boat.

Dan's first glimpse of the dike was of a long ridge of earth about four feet high and ten feet wide built along the riverbank. It stretched upriver farther than he could see.

"You're only seeing the top of the dike," Mr. Edwards explained. "It's really about twenty feet high and near forty feet wide at the base. You can see how high the river has come up."

Opposite them a crew of men were working on top of the dike. As the boat drew nearer Dan could see exactly what they were doing. They were building a row of sand-bags along the top of the dike. It was already several hundred feet long and two bags high.

A dump truck backed along the top of the dike to a group of men. It dumped a load of sand and shot away. The men, all dressed alike in blue shirts and pants and wearing black raincoats and caps or sou'westers, worked in small teams. Two men held a sack open. A third shoveled sand into it. A fourth twisted a piece of wire about the neck, closing it. Then he lifted it to the shoulder of one of three waiting men. He walked out to the line of sacks and added his to the end. Then he returned for another. Other teams were strung out all along the dike doing the same thing. Each group was building a line of sacks that would be united into one long line. Men with rifles stood near each working group watching—the guard.

Dan nosed *Methuselah* in slowly toward the second group of men and watched as one of them heaved a sack onto his shoulder, walked out along the dike and dropped it at the end of the line. He started to turn away, then glanced toward *Methuselah*. Dan suddenly leaned out the window and shouted at the top of his lungs, "Rocky! Rocky! Hey, Rocky!"

Rocky knocked back his sou'wester showing bold sharp features and a streak of straight blond hair. He scowled at the waving boy leaning out the pilothouse window. Then he waved his arm and shouted, "Danny! Hey, Danny Boy!" He stepped over the line of sacks and slid down the short bank to the water's edge. "Danny Boy!" he shouted, "what're you doin' up here?"

Twenty feet offshore Dan stopped *Methuselah* and held her against the pull of the current. "I live near here," he shouted back. "Down the river a ways."

"So this's where you got to. I wondered," Rocky shouted. "What are you doing with the boat?"

"Salvaging logs with Mr. Edwards. How are you doing?"

Rocky spread his hands and grinned, "Well, you see."

A guard came down the bank and took Rocky's arm. He pointed back up the bank. Rocky called, "Be seein' ya, Danny," and turned and climbed the bank.

The guard said, "Shove off, Mister. This is no place for you."

"Just a minute." Mr. Edwards walked up into the bow. "We came up here to check on what's happening to this dike. The radio reports we've been getting don't sound very promising."

The guard nodded. He shifted the rifle to his other hand. "I don't blame you for being worried. I'd be, too, was I you. But you can relax. We've got two hundred men in crews like this stationed the full length of this dike. We've got men walking and inspecting every square foot of it day and night. The minute we find a weak spot we jump on it with a crew. If necessary we can build this breastwork four or five feet high. Go home and get a good night's sleep. We've got everything under control." He grinned and turned and climbed back to the top of the dike.

Dan advanced the throttle and swung *Methuselah* away and downriver again. Mr. Edwards came into the wheelhouse and stood beside him. "So that was Rocky. I always wondered what he looked like."

"Mr. Simmons said he'd make the big pen," Dan said thoughtfully, "and he sure did."

Mr. Edwards looked through the window for a minute then asked, "Do you miss Rocky and the gang, Dan?"

"I did at first. Rocky was good to me. He was the only friend I ever had," Dan said. "I was surprised to see him."

Mr. Edwards nodded. He went back outside, picked up the pike pole and joined Nipper in the bow.

They gathered in five good logs on the way home. When they pulled into the backwater and looked at the flood gauge, the river had risen another foot.

That night the radio news merely mentioned that the upriver dike was holding well. It talked mostly of three downriver towns that had been flooded out. "Private boats of all kinds have been pressed into service as police patrol boats. Their civilian skippers and crews have been deputized and are patrolling the river and towns to keep out looters," the announcer said.

Dan finally went to bed and lay there thinking about Rocky. It was mighty odd how things sometimes turned out. Rocky, who had never worked, but had always ordered the rest of the gang around, was up there carrying sandbags day and night to protect Dan and the Edwards family.

nine

Something wakened Dan. He lay in the darkness of the room and listened. He had cracked the window open for fresh air and he could hear the steady drip of water from the eaves. After a minute he turned over and tried to go back to sleep. He was just drifting off when he heard a muffled sound. He turned on his back and lay listening. Finally it came again. It was low, and sounded like a moan. He thought of the two owls. But this was not owl talk. He sat up in bed. It came again, a little louder, insistent. It came from the barn. It was Junior bellowing, and the barn muffled the sound. He lay down again, thinking, Junior, shut up and go to sleep.

But why would Junior bellow in the middle of the night?

He never had before. It was not his usual kind of mean-sounding bellow. There seemed to be a new note in it. He searched for an explanation and found it when the bull bellowed again. Urgency. Fear. Junior afraid? Of what?

He swung his legs over the side of the bed and went to the window.

It was black dark. He could see nothing. Then he made out the outline of the laying house, the brooder house, and last the barn. He opened the window farther to hear. He felt the damp breath of the rain. The chill of the night cut through his thin pajamas and he shivered. Junior bawled again.

Finally he could see the ground below. It was an odd sort of ground such as he'd never seen before. He leaned out the window, rubbed his eyes, and looked hard. Then he knew, and shock went smashing through him. This was why Junior was bellowing, why there was the note of urgency and fear in his voice. He gripped the window sill unable to believe what he was seeing. Water! It was all around the barn, the laying house. The brooder house was more than half under. Dark and deadly and silent it lapped at the foot of the hill on which the house stood.

Dan dashed from his room, down the stairs, through the kitchen, and hammered on Mr. Edwards' bedroom door. "Mr. Edwards," he shouted. "The dike's broke! We're flooded!" He heard Mr. Edwards' feet hit the floor and turned and ran back through the kitchen. He threw open the door and stepped out on the porch. Nipper rose and came with him. Then Mr. Edwards was beside him in a bathrobe. Together they looked at the water at the foot of the hill. Junior bellowed again.

Mr. Edwards said, "We've got to get the cows out before they drown, if some of them haven't already. Let's go." He ran back to the bedroom to dress. Dan took the stairs two at a time.

He tore out of his pajamas, rushed into his clothes, and bolted back down the stairs. As he entered the kitchen Mr. Edwards came from the bedroom buttoning his shirt. Doris Edwards, in a bathrobe, was right behind him. Behind her mother trooped Jennie, rubbing her eyes, and demanding sleepily, "Hey! What's everybody running around for? We got a fire or something?"

Doris Edwards snapped on the kitchen light and said, "No, a flood." She turned on the radio, then tried the telephone. "Telephone's dead."

Mr. Edwards nodded, struggling into his coat. "That figures. I'll bet the lines are down clear to the city. I wonder where both flashlights are."

Doris Edwards found them and handed one to Dan.

Jennie asked, "Whatcha going to do, Pop?"

"Get the cows out before they drown."

"Can I go too, Pop? I can help."

Mr. Edwards buttoned his coat and took the flashlight. "We don't need help on this. Besides, the water'll be too deep. You stay with your mother."

"Aw, heck!" Jennie pouted. "I never get to do anything exciting."

The radio came on as they went out the door. "The upriver dike went out about 11:00 P.M. The whole valley is flooded. A number of people have not been accounted for. The loss in livestock is expected to be great. There was no warning . . ."

164

Nipper met them on the porch and trotted down the hill beside Dan. Dan followed Mr. Edwards into the water and felt his shoes fill with the first step. He went to his knees, his waist. He caught his breath at the icy shock. Then he remembered this was melted snow water from the high mountains.

Nipper waded up to this chest and began to bark after Dan. Dan called, "Go back, Nipper! Go back to the house. Go back. You hear?"

Nipper backed out of the water and trotted up the hill to the porch.

The water grew no deeper. With flashlight probing the night they waded around the corner of the barn and along the side to the door. Mr. Edwards pulled it open and reached for the light switch. "We don't dare touch the lights," he said. "Just use your flashlight."

The flashlight beams showed Dan the strangest sight he'd ever seen. The main floor of the barn was completely flooded. Bedding straw, hay, a mixture of grain, all floated on top of the water like a thick blanket dotted with empty pails, a couple of boxes, and empty grain sacks. The cows were standing belly-deep in the water. Twenty heads swung toward them and twenty pairs of eyes were big, round, and shiny with fear. An imperative lowing went down the line as though every cow knew that at last help had arrived. From the end of the barn Junior began bellowing loudly.

Mr. Edwards said, "See if Rosie's still alive. If she is, we've got to take care of her first."

Dan waded down past Junior's stall. The bull swung his head and swished water about as he stamped and tried to turn, watching Dan with red-rimmed eyes that showed the white of panic. Dan pulled open the door to the maternity ward and the beam found Rosie standing with just her small head above water. She waded toward him, big eyes rolling in fright, bleating piteously. Dan shouted to Mr. Edwards, "She's all right. But just her head's out."

"Bring her down here. We'll get a rope on her and hoist her into the loft."

Rosie was afraid to leave the maternity ward. Dan had to get behind and push her down the line of cows to Mr. Edwards who waited under the open trap door to the loft.

"You think she'll be safe up there?" Dan asked. "Suppose the barn floats away?"

"It won't. These walls are bolted to the concrete floor. The floor will anchor the whole barn."

They fastened a rope around Rosie's middle, then Mr. Edwards climbed into the loft and hoisted Rosie, kicking and bleating, through the trap door.

Mr. Edwards came back down, dropping the trap door behind him. "Now, let's see if we can get the cows out. We'll take them out behind the laying house and across that low land to the hills. I'll go ahead and lead Junior. The cows will follow him. When I get Junior to the door start letting the cows out. You bring up the rear and see we don't lose any and keep them moving. I don't think the water will get any deeper. Barring an accident we won't have to swim at all. But we'll have about half a mile of water to drive these cattle through. We'll have the south fence to cross. I'll take the wire cutters. All right. I'll get Junior. We'll go through this side door that we came in so we won't be near the pasture. They'll be headed the right direction when they go out the door. If I go too fast, yell. And keep your flashlight burning. It'll help keep them in line."

Mr. Edwards snapped a ten-foot-long chain through the ring in Junior's nose and led him out of the stall. For once Junior was not shaking his head, rattling his chains, and acting mean. He waded along beside the man, making low anxious rumblings, eyes glued to the open side door. He was getting out of here and he knew it.

Dan opened Blossom's stanchion as Junior passed. She turned dutifully and fell in behind the bull. He went down the line snapping other stanchions open. Each cow fell into line as if she understood. They passed out of the barn with a great splashing and swirling of water. Dan pulled the main switch as he left and followed Mr. Edwards and the cows.

Ginger was last out and she, of all the cows, turned and started toward the pasture. Dan waded up beside her, slapped her on the neck and said, "Go on, get back there." She turned back and followed Belle's wake. There was no further trouble.

Dan heard Nipper barking and swung his flashlight beam. The dog was standing with his forefeet in the water. Nipper began wading out toward the cattle. Dan called, "Nipper, go back. Stay there! Stay!" But these cattle were Nipper's responsibility. He kept wading carefully deeper.

Doris Edwards called from the porch, "Nipper! Here, Nipper! Come here, Nipper." Nipper waded on, tail waving, his eyes on the line of cattle filing slowly past.

Jennie ran down the hill sliding and slipping in bathrobe

and slippers. She waded knee-deep into the water. She caught Nipper just as he was beginning to swim, and pulled him back.

The line of cows moved past the dark bulk of the brooder house. Dan was amazed to discover the house was more than two-thirds under water. He listened intently for sounds coming from it. But with the splashing of the twenty cows he could hear nothing. They went close by the laying house and all was quiet within. Dan flashed his light along the front. The water was inside. But the floor was some two feet off the ground and the roosts were about three feet above the floor. The hens, he guessed, must still be all right.

Behind the brooder house they headed straight out toward the south fence and the high land a good half mile beyond. At the head of the line of cows' backs the beam of Mr. Edwards' flashlight lanced across the dark water. Dan barely made out the shape of Junior's head beside Mr. Edwards. The bull was as docile as the gentlest cow. There was not a sound from any of the animals.

It was an eerie, frightening sensation. In all directions there was nothing but flat, dark, mysterious water. It was the darkest hour before dawn and it seemed to Dan they struggled slowly through water and night toward some distant destination they would never reach. The only thing they had to follow was the probing beam of Mr. Edwards' flashlight. The soft rain drifted down and fell silently into the flood. The only sounds were the gurgle of water around the cows' bodies and the deep sighing of their breathing. The only movement was the wavering outline of the backs ahead of him.

Momentarily the water became deeper and Dan sank to his chest. Then it gradually grew shallow until it was again waist-deep. He felt the steady pull of an unseen current. His feet sank into soft earth and the weight of the icy water held him back. His legs turned numb with cold but he kept moving ahead with Ginger's back always before him. He tired and began to pant. Then he became aware of Ginger's labored breathing. The cows, too, were getting tired.

Up ahead Mr. Edwards stopped and the patient line of cattle stopped behind him. Dan knew they had reached the south fence and he was cutting the wire. A minute later they moved forward again. They were in what had been open country now. The tops of brush showed above the water. They no longer traveled in a straight line but detoured around patches of brush which made the way longer. The ground underfoot was uneven. Dan stepped into holes and off the tops of small hummocks that dropped him a foot or two deeper into the water. He was soon soaked to the shoulders. Once he stumbled over a root and went completely under. He gripped the flashlight tightly. It still burned on. Once he tangled in a low-growing bush that barely reached the surface, had to back up and feel his way around. This was the land he had thought was flat when they searched for the lost Beauty across it.

Finally he realized the water was slowly growing shallower. The long lance of Mr. Edwards' flashlight picked up solid earth. Then Mr. Edwards and Junior were on the high ground and the rest of the herd followed. Mr. Edwards unsnapped the chain from Junior's nose, and with the bull leading the way, the whole herd moved gradually off into the night and began feeding.

Mr. Edwards sat down on a rock and said, "I'm bushed. Let's take five before we start back. I never realized before how far a half-mile was."

Dan found a rock and sat down. Off in the near distance Junior began grumbling and rumbling. He was out of the water, no longer afraid, and was his old ugly self again. Dan asked, "Will the cows be all right here? They won't wander off and get lost?"

"They know where home is. They'll be down at the edge of the water waiting to be milked. We'll have to wade out morning and night to milk them."

"What'll we do with the milk?"

Mr. Edwards thought a minute. "We can't carry pails of milk back across this water and we'd have no way of keeping it if we could. The milk truck can't get through. We'll milk them out on the ground by hand."

"That's eighty gallons a day wasted."

"That's right. But at least we saved the herd. I'll bet a lot of dairymen in this valley lost their cattle last night." He stood up and pointed at a gray streak that was spreading to reveal the distant horizon. "Be morning soon. We'd better get back and check the laying house and brooder house. We'll eat breakfast first, then come back here and milk."

It took them just as long to wade back. Before they made it, full dawn was spread gray and soggy across the valley. It disclosed a great body of mud-brown water that reached from the hills behind them to the rock-ribbed battlements that rose dimly in the rainy distance to mark the far side of the river. The current Dan had felt in the dark he now saw. It eddied slowly around unseen objects beneath the water.

It swirled lazily around brush clumps, bending and swaying the stalks. The whole flood moved in a sullen sheet down the valley. The riverbank was no longer visible. But a line of cottonwood, fir, and tall brush marked where it once had been. The only spot of earth rising above this sea was the little mound ahead of them where the house stood completely surrounded by water.

They checked the laying house. The water was a foot deep on the floor. The hens were all huddled on the long roosts that were still almost two feet above the water.

"They're all right for now," Mr. Edwards said. "Let's take a look at the brooder house."

The brooder house was gone. Dan saw it floating off down the pasture turning slowly in a brown current. He started to wade frantically after it but Mr. Edwards called him back.

"It's no use, Dan. We can never catch it."

"But the pullets . . ."

Mr. Edwards said, "They're dead. The roosts were all they had to get on and they were only a couple of feet off the floor. That house is swamped almost to the roof. It only takes a minute or two for a chicken's feathers to become soaked. Then it drowns."

Dan stood there and watched the brooder house float away. He felt sick.

"Come on," Mr. Edwards said, "we'll get some breakfast, then go back and milk."

They were wading out of the water at the foot of the hill when they spied the old rowboat pulled up on the bank. "Looks like somebody's come to check on us," Mr. Edwards said. "Could be Fred Hackett."

"We could take this rowboat and catch the brooder house," Dan said.

Mr. Edwards shook his head. "It's got too big a start on us. And if we did catch it we couldn't hold it against the pull of the current with only a rowboat. It's gone and so are the pullets. Forget it." He started up the hill, water pouring off him. Dan followed.

Nipper was on the porch waiting for them. Dan patted his head and said, "You were a good dog to stay here. You couldn't have helped this time."

They went into the kitchen and stopped. It seemed to Dan that he saw everything at once. There were Jennie and her mother standing across the room by the drainboard. They both looked frightened, and for once Jennie had nothing to say. Her brown eyes were big and round. She looked as though she was about to cry. Doris Edwards' face was white. She stood behind Jennie gripping her shoulders as if she were protecting her. A short, stocky man in a blue shirt and pants, with a thick neck and a great expanse of chest and shoulders, sat in a chair near the table. He held Mr. Edwards' rifle, the one Dan had killed the cougar with, across his knees. His thick finger was on the trigger. Dan noticed automatically that the safety was off. He had the blackest, sharpest eyes Dan had ever seen. His face was broad and tough looking. His bullet head was covered with black hair. A second man stood near the seated one. He was small, almost frail. He wore the same blue shirt and pants. His small head had only a fringe of graying hair around his ears. His eyes were the palest blue Dan had ever seen. They looked enormous behind thick horn-rimmed glasses. He swallowed nervously and his big eyes blinked rapidly at Dan and Mr. Edwards. A third man leaned on a chair back. He smiled and said, "Hiya, Danny Boy. Told you yesterday I'd be seein' ya. Remember?"

Dan stammered, "Rocky! How'd you get here?"

Rocky Nelson was four years older than Dan. He had sharp, thin features with bright eyes that never looked directly at you, and big horsy teeth that showed when he smiled.

Rocky said now: "Easy. When the dike went out everybody started runnin' around hollerin' and yellin'. It was simple for Sam Jacks and Nick and me to just take off. An old tub of a rowboat floated by and we all piled in and headed for here. You told me yesterday you lived about eight miles downriver. When we found that *Methuselah* boat of yours we knew where to go." He spread his hands and showed his big teeth again. "Not bad, huh, Danny Boy?"

Mr. Edwards looked at Sam Jacks holding the rifle and asked angrily, "Just what do you want?"

Jacks shifted the rifle idly so the muzzle pointed at Mr. Edwards' chest. "Easy." His voice was cool and sure. "We need that old powerboat of yours, you, the kid here to run it, and a change of clothes all around." He sized up Mr. Edwards. "I guess the clothes are out. Yours would be too big for any of us. The kid's are too small for me and Jeff and too big for Nick. We'll settle for the boat and you two."

"You fellows are going to try to get away by river?" Dan was amazed at how calm Mr. Edwards' voice was. "You'll never make it. They've got hundreds of boats patrolling the river between here and the city. They're filled with men who've been deputized to stop looting. You'll be picked up in a couple of hours. Your best bet is overland, alone."

Sam Jacks shook his bullet head. "They'll be looking for us walkin' overland. Three men would be stopped right off. That's where you and the kid come in. They expect you to be on the river catching logs. Nobody's gonna stop your boat and question you."

"They'll see you."

"We'll be hiding inside that little cabin. Only you and th' kid'll be in plain sight."

"Hiya, Danny Boy. Told you yesterday I'd be seein' ya. Remember?"

"Where we could signal them or something," Mr. Edwards said.

"Now that'd be downright foolish, wouldn't it?"

Mr. Edwards said nothing and Dan realized he had come to the end of his arguments. Sam Jacks's plan was so simple, so logical, it could not be disputed.

As he listened Dan's mind was racing. It's all my fault, he thought. If I hadn't talked Mr. Edwards into going up there yesterday, if we hadn't seen Rocky, and especially if I'd kept my mouth shut, these men wouldn't have known

where to come. They wouldn't be here frightening Jennie and Mrs. Edwards to death. It's up to me to get them away from here.

But he hadn't the faintest idea what he could do.

"You're elected," Jacks said. "You and the kid and the boat."

Then Dan knew. But he would have to be convincing. Behind Jacks's sharp black eyes lay a cool, calculating mind. There wasn't time to think of the consequences of his decision. There was only time to do it. Jacks was leaning forward to rise.

"Mister," Dan said, "you're crazy to take Mr. Edwards along." He was surprised at how matter of fact he sounded. "What do you want him for? I'm the one you need. I run the boat. Having him along just makes it tougher."

"How so?" The black eyes fastened on Dan with as driving a look as he'd ever known.

"Suppose one of those special sheriff's patrol boats does stop us. He might somehow give us away. Why risk it?"

"If we leave him, he'll be dashing off to call the cops the second we're outta sight."

"This phone's out," Dan said, "it's miles to the nearest neighbor, and the road's under water. He'd have to hike cross-country, and from here he'd have to wade more than half a mile waist-deep and deeper to reach the first solid ground. It'd take him all day to hike to the nearest neighbors and back. He doesn't dare be gone that long."

"Why not?" Jacks's voice was cautious. There was suspicion in his black eyes.

"He's got two women here and this flood's still rising. Besides, he's got about three hundred chickens there in the laying house. If the water comes up much farther he'll have to get them out of there or they'll drown. And he's got twenty valuable cows over on that dry land where we just drove them. He's got to go there morning and night and milk them or those animals will be in an awful mess."

Nick said nervously, "Sam, let's quit th' talkin' and get outta here."

"Relax." Jacks never took his black eyes from Dan. "This kid makes sense if we can believe 'im." His eyes were narrowed with suspicion. "But there's somethin' not right here. I can smell it."

Dan glanced at Rocky. "Didn't he tell you about me?"

"Tell me what?"

"There wasn't time, Sam," Rocky said.

"We'll take time now," Jacks said.

Dan drew a deep breath. He didn't dare look at Mr. Edwards or Jennie or Doris Edwards. He looked straight into Sam Jacks's suspicious black eyes and said, "I was part of the same gang Rocky was. We were in on that super-market holdup together. I drove the car. You think this is my home? A stupid judge stuck me out here. Figured life on a farm would be good for a city kid. That's a laugh. Work from five in the morning till nine or ten at night every day."

"You did not," Jennie said suddenly angry. "I took care of the baby chicks."

"Not for three months you haven't," Dan said.

Jennie started to say more and her mother said quietly, "Jennie, be quiet."

"Playing nurse to a bunch of dumb cows and stupid chickens isn't for me," Dan rushed on. He turned to Mr.

177

Edwards then. "I told you the first morning I wanted nothing to do with a farm. I told her, too," he pointed at Doris Edwards. "But you both had to try. For a lousy three meals a day and a place to sleep you could work me to death."

"Dan," Doris Edwards said in a shocked voice, "you don't mean that."

"He means it!" Mr. Edwards' voice was cold and impersonal. His gray eyes were hard. "I sure missed on you a long ways. I should have taken you back that first morning. You fooled me good."

"Thanks to him," Dan pointed at Rocky. "Remember the advice you gave me the night we were picked up?" He asked Rocky. "You said play along with 'em. Do anything they say. Make it easy on yourself."

Rocky nodded. "I remember."

"Well, I did like you said. But now I'm through." Dan looked directly at Sam Jacks. "I've been wanting to get out of here since the day I came, but there wasn't a chance till you fellows showed up. Now I'm going." He pointed at Mr. Edwards. "But I don't want him along. He'll just be in the way. The first thing he's going to do when we get to the city is hunt up a cop."

"Go ahead!" Mr. Edwards' voice was cold and hard. "I'll be glad to get you out of here. I should have known better than to get talked into taking a kid like you. Once a rotten apple always a rotten apple."

Sam Jacks's black eyes jumped from Mr. Edwards to Doris Edwards to Rocky and back to Dan. He listened, held his finger on the trigger of the rifle, and came to his decision. "All right, kid. We'll try it your way."

"I want to change clothes," Dan said. "I'm cold."

"Sure, make it fast. Rocky, you go with him. Don't try anything cute," he warned Dan.

"When I've got a chance to get out of here?" Dan said and went up the stairs.

Rocky sat on his bed while Dan peeled out of his wet clothes and got into dry ones. Rocky looked at the cougar hide on the floor and said, "Some cat."

"I killed him," Dan said.

"No foolin'?" Rocky was impressed.

"That's right."

"You've gained weight," Rocky observed. "Muscle."

"Like I said, I've been working here. Five in the morning till late at night." There was a stub of pencil on the dresser. If he just dared pick it up and scratch out two words on the dresser top or the side of a drawer. "I'm sorry." But Rocky was watching. His fingers touched the pencil and pushed it away. He concentrated on buttoning his shirt.

"All right, let's go." Dan couldn't resist a single last glance around the room, the old dresser, the bed, the closet with most of his few clothes in it, his cougar rug on the floor. Then he went out.

He didn't hurry going down the stairs. His throat was tight and full and he was afraid if anyone said anything to him he wouldn't be able to answer. He swallowed hard several times. In the kitchen he ducked his head and went hurriedly out the door. But he'd seen the cold, severe look on Mr. Edwards' long, bony face, the sick anguish on Doris Edwards'. Jennie was going to cry.

Outside they ran down the hill to the boat and all piled in. Sam Jacks had Mr. Edwards' rifle.

Nipper charged down the hill, jumped into the boat, and began to lick Dan's face.

Dan started to shove him out and Sam Jacks said, "Hold it, kid. That dog was with you the other day. It'll look good havin' th' dog along. A kid and his dog out salvagin' logs. Peaceful and natural. Let th' mutt come along."

Rocky rowed. He was not good with the oars. They went across the pasture and the tops of the fence posts were out of sight. Only a foot or two of the tallest brush patches were above water. Dan's eyes searched for the floating brooder house but it was gone.

Methuselah was there tied to the dolphin. All the logs were still held in the backwater. That second cable he and Mr. Edwards had added had saved them.

Nipper scrambled over the side first. The rest followed with Dan last. Dan threw the short length of rope he found in the bow around the dolphin and made the rowboat fast. Sam Jacks stood on deck holding the rifle, watching. "When anybody on the river finds a floating, empty boat they always start investigating," Dan explained.

"Okay," Jacks nodded.

Nipper went up into the bow as if they were going out to catch logs. All the rest crowded into the wheelhouse with Dan. "What's th' mutt doin' standin' up there in front?" Jacks wanted to know.

"He always goes up there," Dan said. "He looks for logs."

Jacks said nothing.

Dan pressed the starter and prayed that the motor would not start. It caught with the first try and idled smoothly.

He backed out, swung *Methuselah* into the current and they went booming downstream.

Nick smiled and said, "This's more like it. Boy, oh, boy! Now we're gettin' someplace! This I like!" He rubbed small, delicate hands together. His pale eyes were big and round behind his glasses.

Rocky slapped Dan on the back, showing his big teeth. "Boy, here we go! Just like old times with you doin' th' drivin', eh, Danny Boy?"

"Yeah," Dan said. "Where we going?"

"To the city first," Sam Jacks said peering intently out the window. "I figure it's a perfect time to hit th' city. Everybody's upset and runnin' around, a lotta people homeless and lost. Nobody'll notice us. We oughta be able to catch some foreign freighter easy and get clean outta th' country."

Dan nodded. He looked around as though checking everything. He was really stealing a last look, up across the brown water that had once been the pasture. The old house sat forlorn and lonely, almost lost in the rainy distance.

ten

This was not the same river Dan had known for months.
Now it was a mighty giant on a rampage. The spring runoff, or more than a quarter of a million square miles of
melting snow and winter rains, was pouring through this
gorge in the angriest water Dan had ever seen. It snatched
them into its powerful maw like a chip. Dan could hardly
believe such change, but the evidence was all about. The
bosom of the river was littered with debris that swirled and
bobbed as it rushed headlong to the distant sea.

Dead ahead was the mass of a tree that had been torn
whole from the earth. Stumps bobbed about. A snag rolled
near *Methuselah*'s bow. To their right floated the skeleton

of a bridge. Far out was an inverted V, the roof of a build-ing. A kitchen chair, then a davenport, floated past. Logs dotted the surface. Dan guessed that many of the big upriver rafts had broken up.

Nipper barked like mad each time they passed near a log and kept looking back at Dan. He could not understand why they did not pick them up.

Nick finally said, annoyed, "Make that crazy mutt quit barkin'."

"He always barks at floating logs," Dan said.

"Let him bark," Jacks said. "We want this to look natural."

So Nipper stayed in the bow barking at every log that passed near.

Jacks finally asked, "How's the gas?"

"I'm not sure," Dan said. "Twenty-five or thirty gallons."

"Enough to take us into the city?"

Dan had the feeling that Jacks knew the answer to that question so he said, "No, we'll need gas."

"How come?" Rocky demanded. "It's only about fifty miles or so. The biggest car can go five times as far on that much gas."

Dan spun the wheel and they missed the square floor of a building with bent plumbing pipes sticking through. "You don't get the same mileage with a boat that you do with a car. Wide open, this boat will do about nine knots—a little over ten miles an hour. With the motor turning over at the same speed in a car, you'd be doing around a hundred."

"No kiddin', Danny?"

Dan nodded. The bow bumped something and an instant later a table top bobbed by. "This motor drives a propeller. Wheels are something else."

"So we need gas," Jacks said. "Where do we get it? Some farm?"

"Any farms we can reach will be under water," Dan said. "And they almost always put the gas tanks under ground. It would be flooded. We've got to find a floating marina or something."

"Then we keep lookin'. We got enough gas for four or five hours. That right?"

"Yes."

They passed close beside an immense log rolling sluggishly and Nipper barked frantically.

"I guess you're pretty good with this tub, huh?" Nick asked.

"Pretty good," Dan said.

Nick pointed at a bobbing stump and asked, "What happens if we hit that?"

"We'd likely cave in the bow and sink."

"You got any of them life preserver things on this tub?"

"No."

Rocky laughed. "You scared, Nick?"

"I'll be glad when we're off this boat," Nick said. "I can't swim."

"You hear that, Sam?" Rocky grinned. "Nick can't swim."

Jacks turned his bullet head and said, "Knock it off."

"Sure, Sam. Sure." Rocky looked out the window and said no more.

A good hour had gone by when Dan spotted a big tug

steaming upriver, throwing a V of brown water from her driving bow.

"Down!" Jacks ordered. "Outta sight! Kid, you'd better handle this right."

Nick and Rocky crouched beneath the window at Dan's feet. Sam Jacks was on his knees by the motor, holding the rifle.

The tug came on. A sheet-metal frame was fastened to the bow. It headed for a tangle of debris that had been packed tightly together by the current. It slammed its nose against the bundle and began to push. Boards and timbers snapped. The debris flew apart.

Sam Jacks asked, "What's th' tug up to, kid?"

"It's breaking up debris so it can't smash into something farther downriver."

"They gonna stop us?"

"I can't tell."

The tug came opposite and blew its whistle. A man waved from the deckhouse.

Dan waved back. In the bow Nipper barked.

The man in the wheelhouse laughed and the tug went on.

"It's gone," Dan said.

Nick let out his breath and said, "Man, we gotta get rid of these duds. These blue shirts and pants are a dead giveaway."

"Nick," Rocky grinned, "you worry too much."

"He's right," Jacks said. "Kid, you know of any isolated store along this riverbank?"

"No stores along the riverbank that I know of," Dan said. "But the highway's over there on the left. We can cut across these flooded fields and look for one along it."

"All right, the first place you can get through this rim of brush, head for the highway."

A mile later Dan found a break in the solid line of brush and trees and turned into it. The wall of a building was wedged into the opening. There was barely room to squeeze through.

They came into open, still water beyond. Through the rainy distance Dan saw a house and cluster of farm buildings.

Nick said, "A house. Maybe we can find clothes there."

"We'll look," Jacks said.

Dan steered past a barn and machine shed. A small, square building—a hog house—was jammed against a corner of the machine shed so hard it was stuck there. Dead chickens floated about. The house sat high off the ground. The long porch was only a couple of feet under water. It was jammed with cows standing shoulder to shoulder. They swung their heads toward the boat and began to bawl. An upstairs window rattled open and a man leaned out. He shouted and waved his arms.

"Swing away," Jacks said sharply. "Get outta here."

"He needs help," Dan burst out.

"That's his problem. Keep going."

Dan swung away. He heard the cows bawling for a long time.

A few minutes later Dan spotted the tops of a line of highway signs and followed them. Finally they approached an old red and white store building with a shed roof over a submerged porch.

Jacks studied the store carefully. A few pieces of board

floated around the front with a couple of crates, boxes, and cardboard cartons. The place looked deserted.

"Come up on it slow," Jacks said. "If anybody shows, go on past. Nick! Rocky! get down till we make sure."

Dan advanced slowly. As they drew near he saw through the glass door. Water was halfway up the counters. Merchandise floated in the aisle.

"Okay," Jacks said, "we'll stop. Rocky, tie us to one of those porch posts."

Rocky splashed knee-deep onto the porch and made them fast.

"Let's go in." Jacks started out of the wheelhouse.

"I don't need clothes," Dan said. "No sense me getting soaked."

Jacks nodded. He plucked the ignition key from the lock and dropped it in his pocket. "Nick," he said, "come on."

Jacks smashed the glass in the door and they went in.

Dan squatted on deck and put his arms around Nipper. He knew now that his act back at the farm this morning hadn't been wholly accepted. Sam Jacks trusted no one. He was sure that before they reached the city these men would be involved in more serious crimes than breaking into a country store. He wanted no part of it. He was in enough trouble, having left with them. But there was no chance to get away as long as they were on the boat. Somehow they had to get off *Methuselah*. The only way he knew would be to deliberately wreck her, or if they ran out of gas and had to abandon.

Dan knew he could not deliberately wreck the boat. But she was almost out of gas. That was his one hope. Once on land, Nipper and he would have a chance to slip away. Give them a fifty-foot start in the brush, he thought, and Jacks would never catch them. He didn't have to worry about Nick or Rocky. Nick was frightened and thinking only of himself. Rocky was loudmouthed and stupid. Trying to be funny and fawning around Jacks were his only interests. Dan wondered what he'd ever seen in Rocky.

Rocky waded out, arms loaded with canned goods. "A banquet, Danny Boy," he grinned. He dumped the load on deck and returned inside.

Jacks appeared, carrying a couple of loaves of bread and a box of crackers in one arm, the rifle and a transistor radio in the other. He added all but the rifle to the pile.

Dan began packing the stuff in a corner of the wheelhouse. Jacks and Rocky returned, laden with clothing, and climbed aboard. Jacks yelled, "Come on, Nick."

"Right away," Nick answered. A minute later he splashed out, arms loaded with clothing.

Jacks said, "Close the door. No sense advertising we've been here."

"They'll see the busted window," Rocky pointed out.

"That don't mean anybody's been inside," Jacks said. "Close it."

Jacks returned the key to the ignition and said, "Head for the river."

As they churned toward the brush and trees that marked the river channel Jacks set the radio on the counter, turned it on, and began twisting the dial. In a few seconds he picked up one of Portland's five stations. An announcer was talking about the flood.

"The whole valley is under water. The river suddenly

rose several feet during the night and the upriver dike could not hold the tremendous force of water that struck it. The three upriver towns of Bluff, Riverview, and Stevens are under more than six feet of water. Hundreds of homes lining the riverbanks that lead into the city are flooded or isolated. The loss in livestock will be great. There's no way of knowing yet what the loss in human life will be, but scores of persons are missing."

"That's good for us," Jacks said. "Lots of confusion. Nobody'll pay any attention to us."

The announcer came on again. "It has been reported that three prisoners who were working on the upriver dike are missing. It is not known at this time whether they escaped or drowned. They are Nick St. John, a forger, doing five years; Rocky Nelson, two years, for a supermarket robbery; and Sam Jacks, ten years, for the holdup of the Central Avenue Bank."

"Hey!" Rocky grinned. "We're famous. How about that, Sam?"

Jacks grunted. He shut off the radio. They had almost reached the fringe of brush and trees. Dan was about to ease through into the channel when Jacks said, "Tie up to one of these trees. We'll change clothes and eat."

Dan pulled under the low branches of a fir tree and Rocky made them fast.

The three men skinned out of their prison blues and donned the clothing they'd taken from the store. Tan pants and shirts. Nick had found a cap to cover his bald head. "Man, I feel better," he sighed. "That blue stuff was makin' me nervous."

Rocky had found more. He unfolded a red sport coat and slipped it on. "Hey, Sam," he turned around modeling it. "Sharp, huh?"

"Where'd you find that?"

"In a closet back there," Rocky grinned.

Jacks held out a hand. "Let's see it."

Rocky slipped off the coat and handed it to Jacks. Jacks hurled it out the door into the water.

"Hey!" Rocky dived for the door. Jacks slammed him against the wheelhouse bulkhead. "You stupid clown," he said savagely, "when are you gonna get it through your thick head that this's serious. If somebody sees you wearin' that fancy coat aboard this old tub it'll be like wavin' a red flag. Attention is the one thing we don't want. Understand?"

"Sure. Sure," Rocky said quickly. "I didn't mean anything. Honest."

Jacks pointed at a spare bundle in a corner. "What's that?"

"A change for Danny." Rocky held up a shirt, smiling, trying to divert Jacks' anger from him. "What you think, Sam?"

Dan said quickly, "I'm not wearing them." He didn't want clothing stolen from that little country store. He said to Sam Jacks, "I'm the one any special police or deputies will be seeing. On a boat like this they'll expect me to be wearing old pants and shirt with grease stains and dirt. Brand-new clothes would be as noticeable to an old boatman as that red jacket."

"Put 'em back," Jacks said. "He can wear 'em when we get to the city."

Jacks had Rocky make a bundle of their old uniforms, tie a wrench to it and drop it overboard. Then they sat on deck, hacked open cans of beans and sardines, tore open a loaf of bread and ate. Dan called Nipper in and poured a full can of beans on a piece of paper for him.

When they finished eating Jacks said, "If anybody asks, you live upriver—don't say where. Now, let's measure the gas."

The stick showed about fifteen gallons, enough for two hours' running.

"We need gas," Jacks said, "or we're dead. Everybody keep an eye out for a marina, or a gas tank stuck on stilts, or anything that looks like it might have gas in it. All right, let's go."

Dan backed off from the tree and headed for the hole in the brush. Nipper trotted up into the bow again.

They cruised for almost an hour. The amount of debris increased. Dan spotted a low floating building that looked like the Edwards' brooder house, but he didn't get close enough to make sure. They passed a chicken house, the roof all but awash. A line of chickens perched precariously on the ridge. Dan guessed they must have less than ten gallons now. In another hour that would be gone and they'd have to take to the land.

They rounded a bend. To the left a small dock lifted its floor several feet above the flood. Behind the dock there was a cluster of homes set in the pattern of streets. Water was halfway to the roofs of the houses. A sign above a flooded gas station read Riverview. Two powerboats cruised among the houses. A third boat was in the channel no more than two hundred yards off. Dan saw two men inside the wheelhouse. Another in slicker and sou'wester stood in the bow holding a rifle.

"Everybody down!" Jacks dropped below the window line. "Kid! don't let those guys come aboard." He crouched at Dan's feet, the rifle in his hands.

The patrol boat bore down upon them. The man in the bow held up his hand for Dan to stop.

"They want me to stop," Dan said.

"Slow down, don't stop," Jacks cautioned.

The patrol boat pulled alongside a few feet away. The man in the bow called, "You got business on this river, boy?"

"Yes, sir. I'm salvaging logs."

"You're pretty young to be out here alone."

"Tell 'im you're seventeen," Jacks whispered, "that you've been handling a boat since you were twelve."

Dan told him. He gauged the distance between them. He could jump and land on that deck. But the man held his rifle loosely, obviously not ready for trouble. Beneath him Jacks was ready. He didn't dare risk it.

The man said, "You're pretty young. You got a salvage license?"

"Tell 'em your old man has," Jacks whispered.

Dan repeated it. The man asked next, "What do you do with the logs?"

"They're auctioned off. Dad gets 60% for his work."

Dan heard the man at the wheel say, "That's right, Bob."

But Bob was not satisfied, "I haven't seen you or your boat before."

"We're from upriver a few miles," Dan said.

The man at the wheel said, "He's all right, Bob."

Bob said, "Okay, son. But be careful." The boat swung away and went plowing upriver.

"Whew!" Rocky said. "That was close, Danny."

"Yes." Dan felt shaky and his palms were wet.

Nick's eyes were enormous. "For Pete's sake, let's quit this squirrelin' around on the river. If them guys had come on board we'd have been sunk."

"They didn't come on board," Jacks pointed out.

"They could have, and the next ones might. I don't like being trapped on a cracker box like this."

"You think we'd do better on land?"

"You can run. You can hide. Every patrol boat that sees us is gonna ask questions. The closer we get to the city the more boats there'll be. Our luck's got to run out."

"The more boats the better," Jacks explained. "We'll be just another boat amongst hundreds—too many to stop and question. We stick with the boat."

"Not me. Next time we get close to land I'm takin' off."

"You're staying," Jacks said evenly.

"You guys don't need me."

"You'd be picked up sure," Jacks said. "Next thing you'd be telling them about us."

"No, I wouldn't."

"I think you would. We stick together until we leave the boat. Then if you wanta take off, okay."

Nick stared out at the brown flood and said nothing.

They cruised along for minutes. They passed a half dozen timbers that were bolted together. A cat sat resigned in the center, cold, wet, and miserable. Rocky laughed, "That old cat'll need all nine lives to get outta this."

Jacks said, "Measure the gas again."

Rocky put the stick inside the tank and said, "We're down to a little over an inch. That's less than eight gallons." For the first time he sounded concerned. "We've got about enough for another hour."

"Can we save any by slowing down more?" Jacks asked.

"I don't dare," Dan said. "I've got to go faster than the current to keep steering. Any slower we'll be drifting the same speed as the current and something'll hit us."

"Then we'd better find gas quick."

In the next half hour they passed three more patrol boats. But they were not challenged.

Dan was counting the minutes and mentally measuring the gas. It wouldn't be long before they'd have to run ashore. Nipper and he were going to get their chance to escape. He said finally, "We'd better head for land before we run out of gas here and drift helpless."

"That's fine by me," Nick said.

"I don't want to drift in the middle of this flood," Rocky said worried.

Jacks scowled, "Get around that bend, then head for shore."

They rounded the bend and Dan pointed *Methuselah*'s bow toward the brush. With a shock he realized he was heading dead on to a floating marina. He saw a huge gas tank on a float and a hose coiled on a bracket. He felt sick.

"Wow!" Rocky showed his big teeth in a grin. "What luck!"

Nick scowled and said nothing.

"Ease up careful," Jacks directed. "Let's see if anybody's there."

Dan came in close to the float. It looked deserted. He reversed the motor and held *Methuselah* against the current.

"Hose is locked with a padlock," Jacks said. "Got a hammer?"

"In that tin box in the corner."

"Good. I can bust the lock."

Nick said nervously. "It'll take time to fill the gas tank. We can't lay here in broad daylight. Somebody'll spot us."

"We've got to chance it," Rocky said.

Jacks's black eyes were darting about. "Pull in behind that brush and trees. We'll wait till dark. Then come and load up."

The brush screen was very thick. Dan could barely see through to the main channel. He could not see the marina float.

"How much farther to the city?" Rocky asked.

"About twenty-five miles," Dan said.

"Sam," Nick asked worried, "you gonna bust right down th' middle of this river into th' city in broad daylight?"

Jacks shook his head. "We'll dodge around from here on. Go down backwaters and sloughs and across fields in daylight runnin'. We'll only go into the channel when we have to. When we get close to th' city we'll run only at night."

They settled down to wait for the daylight hours to pass. Dan called Nipper in and fed him again. Then he sat with his back against a bulkhead and tried to rest. Nipper stretched out beside him and went to sleep. Nick and Rocky lounged across from him. Jacks sat almost under the

195

steering wheel, the ever-present rifle across his knees. At long intervals Dan heard the deep throb of a tug's motor. Once he thought he heard voices. Water gurgled around the tree trunks. A plane went over low and they all looked up, listening. Some floating object went bump-bumping along the side. Toward evening the rain stopped. They ate again and darkness spread across the water. Fog banners drifted in. There were no stars or moon.

Jacks tossed the empty sardine and bean cans overboard and said, "Let's head for that marina."

Dan felt his way into the river's channel and headed upstream. It took all *Methuselah*'s power to buck the current. Running in the dark was a frightening sensation. He could not see objects until he was almost upon them. The V of a roof went past. A dark mass of debris nearly trapped them, but by sliding in close to the brush and trees he avoided it. They had almost made the marina when something struck the bow a hard, glancing blow. *Methuselah* shook and heeled over sickeningly.

Nick yelled in panic, "We're gonna sink! We're gonna sink!"

"Shut up," Jacks said. "Rocky, see if we got any damage."

Rocky went forward, looked and came back. "No damage," he announced. "You can relax, Nick."

Dan knew they'd been lucky.

They pulled in at the marina's dock and Rocky made them fast. With the hammer Jacks broke the lock on the hose. They stretched out the hose and shoved the nozzle into the boat's tank. Maybe, Dan thought, with a last thin hope, the marina tank's empty. But when Rocky pulled the trigger, gas rushed out. Rocky grinned, "Danny Boy, we're in business."

"Yeah," Dan said.

They had just finished filling the tank when Dan heard the deep throb of a motor. The black bulk of a big tug rounded the bend and bore down upon them. Jacks shut off the gas and jumped aboard. "Get going, quick!" he said harshly. "Head for the trees."

Dan made a sharp turn and under Jacks' black eyes yanked the throttle full open. They made it over halfway to the brush when a powerful beam probed the night. It caught them full in its glare and a voice magnified a hundredfold by a bull horn bellowed across the water, "Hold up! Hold up for identification."

"Keep goin'!" Jacks ordered.

The voice filled the night. "Hold up! Hold up or we'll fire on you."

"Dodge left and right," Jacks directed. "Shake that light."

Dan spun the wheel. *Methuselah* heeled to starboard, motor roaring. He swung back to port. They lost the light. It went searching across the littered water. A few seconds later it pinned them again in its blinding glare. The bull horn bellowed, "Hold up or we fire!"

On the heels of that warning came the crack of a rifle. Slivers flew off the bow barely missing Nipper. Dan yelled, "Nipper come in here! Come here!" The dog trotted into the wheelhouse. A second bullet tore into the bow where he'd been standing. The black line of the trees crawled toward them with terrible slowness.

"We ain't gonna make it," Nick wailed. "We ain't gonna make it!"

"Dodge again," Jacks' voice was calm. "They're not gaining. They're shooting to try to stop us. Dodge, kid!"

Dan dodged and lost the light. The bull horn kept booming. The light hit them. A bullet exploded a fountain of water beside the boat. Dan dodged. The light found them just as they made the brush and tree line. Then they were beyond. The light probed among the tree trunks but could not penetrate to them.

Jacks said, "Kill the motor so they can't hear. Everybody quiet."

Dan shut off the motor and they drifted. They heard voices on the tug. "We can't follow in there. It's too shallow."

"We scared 'em off," another voice said. "That'll have to do. Some punks trying to swipe a little gas. Let's go on."

The tug turned away.

Through the thick screening Dan saw the spotlight beam go downriver.

Nick kept mumbling, "That's too close! Too close! I told you, on a boat you ain't got a chance."

Rocky said, "Oh, shut up! You're not hurt. We got away. Sam, what do we do now?"

"It's too dangerous to run at night without a light. We'll tie up to one of these trees and wait for daylight. When we reach those homes near the city the radio told about, we'll see if we can find a good flashlight, so's we can run at night."

They tied to a tree, shut off the motor and sprawled about in the small wheelhouse, trying to rest.

Dan sat with Nipper beside him. He pulled up his knees and bent his head forward as though half asleep. But he was thinking. He wondered what the Edwardses were doing. Jennie might be working on her math. Mrs. Edwards might be knitting on that sweater, or maybe helping Jennie. Mr. Edwards would likely be reading an old paper or magazine, or watching the flood water, or checking on the laying house or on Rosie in the barn loft. But that was a hundred years ago—and he was here in a black world of water with three hunted fugitives, a fugitive himself now.

eleven

Dan slept the sleep of exhaustion for an hour or two. But his cramped position and the cold night air blowing through the open door wakened him. He lay there, his arm around Nipper feeling the warmth of the dog's body. He shivered and moved his stiffened legs. It was very quiet. Through the window he saw the black night sky. There were no stars. *Methuselah* lay utterly still on the flood. Across from him Nick and Rocky slept, each curled up on the deck. Jacks sat almost under the steering wheel, back against the bulkhead. His bullet head was sunk forward. Dan watched the steady rise and fall of the man's chest. He seemed to be sleeping.

This was the first time since they'd left the farm that

Dan wasn't under those watchful black eyes. If it weren't so far to shore and the water so deep, he might slip over the side and get away. But he couldn't leave Nipper. He was thinking of the dog and looking idly at the motor when he remembered how Nipper had broken the rotor and almost drowned Mr. Edwards.

The thought came with a suddenness that startled him. If he could loosen one of the distributor clamps and twist the cap ever so little, then tomorrow morning, the moment he pressed the starter, it would break the rotor. That would be as good as running out of gas. Jacks would never suspect. With four men in this little wheelhouse anyone could have brushed against the cap and knocked it out of line.

The motor was less than six feet away. It would take but a second to unclamp and move the cap. He watched Jacks closely for several minutes. Then he lifted his arm carefully from Nipper's neck. He worked first one leg then the other under him. He rose slowly, never taking his eyes off Jacks. He stepped silently down to the motor, eased a clamp loose and twisted the cap slightly. His head was partially turned, when out of the corner of one eye he caught the movement as Jacks shifted a thick hand on the rifle stock.

Dan froze. Through the dark he felt those black eyes watching him. Fear surged through him and his hands began to shake. But a part of his mind said, "Keep cool. Go right on. You've got to carry it off now."

He loosened the other clamp, acting like he was trying to be quiet, but not too quiet. He removed the rotor and turned. Jacks head was up. He was looking at him.

"Oh," Dan kept his voice low, "did I wake you?" He was surprised at how calm he sounded. Jacks said nothing and he went on, "I couldn't sleep and I remembered this rotor. The dog ran into the distributor a couple of months ago and broke it. I had to put in an old discarded rotor. It's loose, so every couple of days I check it and file the points. I just remembered I hadn't done it. As long as I couldn't sleep I thought I might as well do it now. If this quits out there in the river, it'd be as bad as running out of gas." With the flashlight he rummaged through the toolbox for a file. He said, "You mind holding the light for me while I file these points?"

Jacks held the light and Dan bent over the distributor and carefully filed the points. He cleaned the rotor with a rag and replaced it. He wiggled it to show Jacks how loose it was. He replaced the cap and fastened the clamps. "That ought to do it for a couple more days," he said.

Jacks snapped off the flashlight and sat down under the steering wheel again.

Dan sat beside Nipper. He drew up his legs and bent forward, his head on his knees. The palms of his hands were wet and his insides were jumping. He could feel those black eyes boring into him. He gripped his knees hard to keep from shaking.

He did not sleep again. He heard Nipper get up, click outside and walk about the deck. First dawn came, cutting a slash across the night, and they began to stir. Dan looked at the height of water on the tree trunks and tried to gauge whether it had risen. It seemed about the same.

Nick rubbed his eyes and grumbled, "Man, I hope I don't spend another night on this lousy tub. I ache all over."

"Me, too," Rocky said.

They ate beans and sardines again and Rocky made a face. "I could do without these, too."

Jacks scooped beans from a can and said, "When we get to the city tonight you can have a steak with all the fixings."

Dan glanced at Jacks. The man had had no sleep for two nights that he knew of. Yet he looked clear-eyed and fresh.

"It takes money for steaks," Rocky pointed out.

"We'll get it at those big homes we'll be coming to."

"What time will we reach the city?" Nick asked eagerly.

"Late. We're going to take it slow and careful from here on. We'll do the last few miles after dark."

"Why then?" Nick asked.

"There won't be so many patrol boats out at night, no planes or choppers. We'll look like a patrol boat in the dark."

"Just so we get there," Nick said.

Dan fed Nipper a can of beans again. Rocky watched the dog eating and asked, "What'll we do with th' mutt when we get to th' city? Knock 'im in th' head?"

"Leave him in the boat," Dan said, suddenly angry.

"He's no good to us."

"He is now," Jacks said. "He comes in handy, standing out there where everybody can see him. A kid and his dog on a boat. It looks right and legitimate. We'll worry what to do when we get to the city. Now let's get moving. Not many'll be out this early. We'll go right down the channel till we hit traffic."

The river looked as it had yesterday, brown and swift and vicious, littered with a conglomeration of articles racing to the sea.

They went flying downriver, keeping close to the brush line. They passed the small town of Bluff. A single outboard carrying two men cruised among the half a hundred flooded homes. A couple of miles farther on they spotted two patrol boats across the river. Then one came directly toward them.

All three fugitives ducked below the window line. The boat passed within fifty feet. The man at the wheel waved. Dan waved back.

"It's time to get out of the channel," Jacks said.

Dan found a hole through the brush and trees and they left the river for the flooded fields. They cruised slowly, following the direction of the river.

A helicopter popped from behind distant hills and circled them. Jacks said, "I'll steer. You step out and wave."

Dan did and Nipper barked. The machine was so low Dan could see the pilot wave back. Then he went off across the river.

"You think he's satisfied?" Nick asked.

"He waved," Jacks pointed out. "He left."

"On th' ground he'd never seen us," Nick worried.

"When we get to the city," Jacks said, "you're on your own."

"Nick, your bellyachin' makes me sick," Rocky said angrily. "Maybe we oughta throw you overboard."

"You know I can't swim."

"That's what I mean."

"All right!" Jacks said. "Knock it off."

They went on, carefully cruising the backwater. Sea gulls sailed low over them, hunting food. One landed on a stump ahead and stood balancing, wings spread. A pair circled a slatted crate, crying and diving.

Jacks turned on the radio. An announcer was giving the latest flood news. "The flood has crested and is no longer rising. So far, twenty-two persons are missing. This includes three prisoners who had been working on the upriver dike. It is believed the prisoners drowned, for they were last seen in a very precarious spot on the dike."

"We're dead," Rocky laughed. "How's it feel to be dead, Nick? That's good, huh, Sam?"

"It gives us a break. But don't fool yourself. They'll still be looking for us; only not quite so hard."

Midmorning they came to a house sitting in a grove of fir trees. They worked the boat around to the side where Jacks broke a window and they climbed through. This time Dan went along.

The water was almost waist deep. Chairs floated about, along with a couple of small tables. The television had been placed on top of the living room table. They waded from room to room, pulling open drawers, dumping them, searching for anything of value. Blankets and pillows floated in the bedroom. Rocky added to the destruction by dumping drawers into the water in his search.

The only thing they took from the house was a small flashlight.

They cruised on. The distant hills began to squeeze in, forcing the flood back toward the main river channel. Finally they stopped behind a brush screen and Jacks studied the channel. They were much closer to the city now. An outboard snarled upriver carrying three men. It was obviously a patrol boat. They waited until it was out of sight then Jacks said, "All right, open her up. Let's get past this narrow spot and see if we can find another wide place to get out of the channel."

They went flying downstream at full throttle. A couple of miles farther the hills fell back. The flood spread out with them. They left the channel for the quiet backwater.

"How much more of this fast water business we got?" Nick asked.

"The last ten miles or so," Jacks said.

"And we'll travel it all in th' dark?"

"That's when it's safest."

Nick adjusted his glasses and stared out the window.

They crossed a wide expanse of water and came upon two large homes sitting side by side up against the fringe of brush that marked the channel.

At the first house Jacks again broke a side window. They searched the house and found nothing of value to them. At the second they found a chest of silverware that Jacks said he could sell.

The hills closed in and they were forced back toward the main river channel again. A long, low bluff ran sheer beside them. They found a home backed against the bluff wall. The water was a third of the way up the main floor windows.

Jacks broke down the side door. "We've got to have something we can turn into cash. Look close."

Again they found a house that seemed to be stripped of everything but the furniture. Dan was in a bedroom pretending to search, when Rocky yelled from the service room. "Hey, come look!" He waded down a hall and found Rocky and Jacks inspecting an immense flashlight.

"This's what we need," Jacks was saying. "It'll throw a light five- or six-hundred feet. We'll tie it on top of the cabin and when it gets dark we'll breeze right down the river into the city and nobody'll ask a question."

They found nothing more, so with Jacks carrying the flashlight, they waded to the side door and got aboard *Methuselah*. Nick was not there and Jacks yelled inside, "Nick, come on!" When there was no answer he said, "Rocky, get him. We've got to get out of here."

Rocky waded through the house calling. A couple of minutes later he was back. "He's gone and th' back door's open. You can wade out about twenty feet and there's a trail leadin' to th' top of th' bluff. He's sneaked off. Do we go after him?"

Jacks's face was ugly, his black eyes narrowed to slits. "Let him go. He'll start writing checks again and get picked up in a few days. That's always the way it goes with him. Let's get outta here."

Dan worked *Methuselah* into the trees and brush that lined the channel, until they were well hidden. He shut off the motor and they watched the fast-flowing current. It seemed to Dan there was a little less debris. He remembered the radio had said that the flood had crested, so that explained it. But there was more river traffic. Far out two coast guard cutters cruised slowly side by side.

"How much farther to the city?" Rocky asked, "eight or ten miles?"

"About that, I'd guess," Dan said.

Jacks said, "They brought us up a road along here when we went to the dike. As I remember, these hills and the bluff stay close to the river. We have to stick to the channel from here on. That means we're through with daylight running. We wait for dark. Let's fix that flashlight for night running."

It took but a few minutes to tie the flashlight to the wheelhouse roof. They opened cans and ate again. Dan called Nipper in and fed him. Then they settled down to wait out the daylight hours.

A plane went over, low and close up to the bluff. A little later a helicopter passed over them. It turned and came back. Rocky muttered without opening his eyes, "You think they've got Nick already and he's blabbed?"

"They're just being careful. We're close to the city."

Evening came. They ate again and Rocky muttered, "This's th' last of th' beans and sardines. My next meal's gonna be a steak two inches thick."

"After we get some money, or something we can turn into money," Jacks said. "We've got to find that between here and the city."

Darkness closed down. Traffic on the river ceased and the complete silence of night settled in. At Jacks's orders Dan backed *Methuselah* out of the brush and worked his way through an opening into the channel. Rocky switched on the flashlight. It threw a powerful beam several hundred feet ahead. The hard pull of the current caught them and Dan swung the boat downstream. He was sure now there was less debris, but he was still kept busy dodging stumps, logs, furniture, and chunks of buildings which the spotlight picked up.

Soon they began to pass big, sprawling, dark homes with glassed-in porches and patios. Water licked at the foundations of some, and was halfway up the windows on others.

Jacks had Dan slow down so he could study the houses. Each time they came to one where it was possible to pull in behind screening brush, or behind the house where they could hide the boat, he had Dan stop. In the next two hours they entered four homes and found nothing. Dan could see a tightening about Jacks's mouth. Rocky said, "Nothin' in all these places. I don't get it."

"There's plenty," Jacks said, "but it's all big stuff. We've got to have things we can carry, that we can put in our pockets. The owners took what they could carry, too, when they ran."

Traffic increased again. At intervals they passed other boats in the dark. A road ran on the edge of the low bluff above and they saw car lights. "Getting awful close to the city," Jacks said and continued to study each home as they passed.

They rounded a bend and saw a big house blazing with light. As they came opposite, a young girl rushed out the door, jumped into the river to her knees and began waving frantically. A man and woman followed. The man waded waist deep beyond the girl and shouted words Dan could not understand.

Without thinking Dan spun the wheel and turned in. He glanced apprehensively at Jacks. "They need help," he said. "They're trapped."

Jacks was looking up at the house intently. "All right," he said surprisingly, "let's take 'em off." He glanced at Dan and Rocky. "Watch your talk. Hear?"

Dan cut the gas and drifted in. The current was not strong close to the bank. The man waded to his chest and clutched the side of the boat. He was about sixty, Dan guessed. He had a refined face and thinning iron-gray hair. "Thank God you came by!" he panted. "The flood undermined our road and it caved in about an hour ago. If you'll take us downriver a mile to higher ground, we can climb up to the highway and get a lift." He saw Jacks holding the rifle and added, "You're the first patrol boat we've seen all evening."

Jacks said, "Ease in to the bank, kid. Rocky, tie us to that tree in front of the porch."

The moment Rocky made them fast the girl waded out, holding up her hands. Dan pulled her aboard and Nipper sniffed at her. She was about fourteen and she tossed her blonde hair back and smiled. "Gee, thanks! We certainly are lucky you came along." Her voice was alive and excited.

The man carried the woman out and Rocky helped them aboard.

Dan was ready to back off and head downriver when Jacks said, "Mister, hadn't you better lock your house and turn off the lights?"

"Of course," the man said. "I forgot."

The woman said, "I left the wall safe open in the dining room, Ralph." She smiled at Jacks. "I got so excited when I saw your boat turn in."

"We'll help you lock up," Jacks said. "Rocky, you stay with the boat. Come on, kid."

Dan hesitated.

"Come on," Jacks said.

The man led the way into the house and headed directly for the dining room. Jacks and Dan were at his heels. Dan knew that something was about to happen, but it came with such brutal suddenness there was no chance to warn the man. Jacks lifted the rifle and smashed it down on his head. He collapsed without a sound.

Dan watched, numb with horror, as Jacks rifled the man's pockets and extracted a roll of bills. Then he hauled Dan into the living room to a small wall safe that stood open. His big hand dug into the safe and piled watches, bracelets, a couple of necklaces, a diamond pin of some sort on the table. For the first time Jacks was excited.

"Man! Man! We hit the jackpot. Look at this! Just look at it. And money, too." He slapped Dan on the back. "Kid, we're in. This's it. We've made it!" He piled the jewelry and money into a napkin, pulled up the corners and stuffed it into his pocket. "Let's get outta here. Come on. Come on!"

Dan looked at the man crumpled on the floor, a thin stream of blood running from a gash in his head. "What, what about him?" he stammered. "He—he might be dead."

"Then let's get outta here." Jacks grabbed his arm and never had Dan felt such a powerful grip. "Keep your mouth shut! Understand? I'll do the talking when we get to the boat. Now move!" He shoved Dan into the hall.

Back on board Jacks explained in a calm voice to the woman and girl, "He had some extra things he wanted to do, so we'll take you downriver a ways and let you off, then come back for him. It ain't safe to leave a boat layin' here. Something might smash into it and sink it."

"I thought he was just going to lock the doors and turn out the lights," the woman said.

"He thought of some other things, papers and such," Jacks said.

"Oh," the woman said. "Yes, of course."

They were all crowded into the wheelhouse on the short run downriver. The girl stood beside Dan. She asked, "Do you know where to let us off?"

"No, you'll have to tell me." Dan kept thinking of her father back at the house. He had to be dead.

Several minutes later the girl said, "Turn in here. There should be a tree sticking out of the water. There's a trail just above it that leads up to the highway."

Dan went in slowly and eased *Methuselah's* bow against a half submerged tree trunk. Rocky went aft, grabbed a limb, and held the stern against the pull of the current. Jacks helped the woman onto the tree trunk and then to shore.

The girl said to Dan, "Thanks. Thanks a lot." She leaped lightly to the tree trunk and ran ashore.

The woman called, "You'll go after my husband?"

"He'll meet you up at the highway," Jacks said. He motioned to Dan. "Back off."

Dan put *Methuselah* in reverse and backed away. The spotlight beam picked up the woman and girl climbing the bank. They broke over the top and disappeared.

Dan knew that Jacks did not intend to go back.

A diamond-bright shine caught his eyes. The pike pole on the roof had been moved and the flashlight beam was shining on its needle-sharp point. A weapon—a deadly, spear-like weapon. They were not going back for the man, because Jacks had killed him. Jacks was turning away from the bow. Dan kept looking at the pike pole point. He began to shake.

He kicked *Methuselah* out of gear, stepped outside, jerked the pike pole off the roof and jammed the point against Jacks's broad chest. It happened so quickly Jacks was caught in midstride. He just stood there, a shocked, unbelieving look spreading across his wide face.

"Don't move," Dan said harshly, "or I'll shove it through you."

Jacks looked down at the sharp point pricking his shirt front, then up at Dan. There was no fear in his face.

Behind Dan, Rocky's shocked voice said, "Hey, Danny, what gives?"

"Stay back!" Dan didn't dare take his eyes off Jacks. "Keep your hands down," he warned. "Drop the rifle."

The rifle clattered on the desk. Jacks's voice was calm. "I wondered about you all along."

Rocky's feet moved softly. Dan said, "Stand still, Rocky, or Sam gets it." The feet moved again, closer.

Nipper stood there, head cocked, taking it all in. Rocky's feet moved again and Dan said suddenly, "Nipper, take him!" He twitched his head back toward Rocky. It was an order the dog understood. He went after Rocky, as he would for a cow that had got out of line. He was a black streak, teeth bared, a growl rumbling in his throat. Behind Dan a startled yell was chopped off in a splash. Rocky was overboard.

Dan concentrated on Jacks. "Take that jewelry out of your pocket and drop it on the deck. Careful!"

Jacks withdrew the napkin and dropped it. "You're making a big mistake," he said quietly. "I know how to get rid of this stuff. You don't."

Rocky's voice yelled in panic, "Sam! Sam! help! Th' dog . . . !"

"It's going back!" Dan said.

213

"So now what?" Jacks asked. "You can't hold that sticker on me all night."

Dan heard Rocky threshing astern. He heard Nipper growl. He gripped the pike pole so tight his muscles began to tremble. "Jump!" he said harshly. "It's only a few feet to shore. Jump!"

"W-h-a-t!" Jacks made as if to start forward and Dan twitched the pole. He could tell by the expression on the man's face he'd pricked the skin.

"Jump!" Dan repeated. "Now!"

Jacks' face turned ugly, the black eyes narrowed as his calm deserted him. He leaped backward suddenly, away from the pike pole point. His right hand slashed down and caught the pole. He held on as he went under.

Dan was yanked powerfully forward. Before he could let go he was jerked overboard. He bobbed up immediately. Jacks was twenty feet away swimming toward the boat. Dan was closer. He reached *Methuselah* in a flurry of strokes, heaved himself aboard and scrambled for the rifle. When he whirled and pointed it, Jacks was only an arm's length away. "Swim for shore," Dan panted. He pressed off the safety. "Swim for shore!"

Jacks looked into the muzzle of the rifle. Then he turned and swam for the bank.

Dan looked for Nipper. He was nowhere on board. There was splashing astern. He ran into the wheelhouse and brought *Methuselah* around. The beam picked up Rocky and Nipper fighting in the water. Rocky was trying to swim

"Jump!" Dan repeated. "Now!"

and keep the dog off. Nipper was after him, growling, every tooth shining.

A log shot into the light rolling sluggishly. It struck dog and man solidly and rode them under. Dan swung the bow of the boat, and the light followed the speeding log. He drew abreast of the log, holding his breath as he searched for Nipper and Rocky. A black something bobbed to the surface. He kicked the boat out of gear and ran to the side. It was Nipper. Dan leaned over and grabbed, just as the dog started to sink again. Rocky was nowhere in sight.

Dan got Nipper on board. He knelt, holding the soaked, battered body in his arms. Nipper was limp. There was no sign of life. "Nipper!" he whispered. "Oh, Nipper!" This, with the past two days of uncertainty, fear, and worry, was more than he could bear. He began to cry.

A cross current caught *Methuselah*, swung her slowly and carried her back to the bank, where she grounded lightly in the dirt. A minute later there was a step on deck. Dan looked up through his tears into the face of a state policeman.

twelve

Officer Rankin knelt on the deck beside Dan and said, "Give me the dog, son."

He stretched Nipper out. His hands kneaded gently; they turned him and worked him. He pried the dog's mouth open and a great quantity of water ran out. Finally Nipper groaned and opened his eyes. He vomited more water. The officer lifted him to his feet. Nipper staggered. He shook himself weakly. He waved his tail and licked Dan's face. Dan hugged him. The officer said, "He was just water-logged."

The officer gathered up the jewelry and watches and put them in his pocket.

"That was stolen from a house about a mile up the river," Dan said.

"I know. My partner and I met the two women when they climbed the bank. We'd been there for an hour, stopping traffic because of the road washout. Lucky you had that flashlight fastened to the roof. We saw everything that happened on the boat. It was a nervy thing you did."

"They were two of the prisoners that escaped when the upriver dike went out," Dan said. "Sam Jacks got away. I'm afraid Rocky Nelson drowned."

"We got Jacks when he came ashore. My partner's holding him."

"He killed the man where he stole that jewelry," Dan said.

"Let's go see. Can you run the boat back up there?"

It took but a few minutes to return to the big house. It was still brilliantly lit. They tied to the same tree and went in. The man was not lying on the dining room floor as Dan had expected. They found him in the bathroom washing blood from a gash in his head. Officer Rankin returned the valuables. They helped him lock up the house, then took him downriver to join his wife and daughter.

As they left the man asked, "You're not going to do anything to this boy, are you? None of this was his fault. I've heard about those three prisoners."

Officer Rankin shook his head, "There's nothing to worry about, Mr. Wright. We just want Dan's full story."

Dan and Officer Rankin went downriver in *Methuselah* to a temporary command post the state police had set up in one corner of a highway restaurant.

Dan told the officer everything, about being a parolee

living with the Edwards family. He explained how the three prisoners had come in on the family, what had happened along the way, the break-ins, and the escape of Nick St. John.

When he finished Rankin made phone calls until he found Hank Simmons. He repeated the story to Simmons. Then he handed the phone to Dan. "He wants to talk to you."

Simmons said, "Dan, this's the darnedest thing. You okay?"

"I'm fine," Dan said. "I want to take the boat back home."

"Sure. Anything else?"

"Yes sir." Dan swallowed and licked his dry lips. "Can you find me another place to stay?"

There was a silence, then, Simmons asked, "Changed your mind?"

"They have," Dan said.

"I can't believe it. What happened?"

"Just find me another place right away." Talking about it was like probing an open wound.

"All right," Simmons said. "I'll be up as soon as this water goes down. Now put the officer back on the phone. And don't worry about anything."

When Rankin hung up he typed a letter, put it in an envelope, and handed it to Dan. "If anybody stops you, this will get you by. Simmons says I'm to give you anything you want."

"I might need a little more gas."

"What else?"

"All Nipper and I have had is beans and sardines for two days."

They went to the restaurant counter and Rankin said, "Marie, the biggest steak in the house with all the trimmings, and fix a bag of good scraps for the best darned dog I've ever seen."

"Coming right up," Marie smiled.

Dan looked at the huge steak and thought of Rocky. This was supposed to be his meal tonight.

Afterward they carried cans of gas to the boat.

Rankin took the silverware, clothing, radio, and big flashlight from the roof. "I'll find the owners. You're not going back tonight?"

"I'll wait till daylight."

Rankin nodded. "Good luck. Be careful."

Dan sat on the deck in the wheelhouse with Nipper beside him and tried to sleep but too many things had happened the last two days. He dozed and woke and dozed again.

The moment first dawn cracked the solid black and he could see the dull surface of the river, he pulled into the channel and headed back upriver. There was definitely less debris today and he thought the current was a little less swift.

They cruised steadily upriver hugging the brush line, avoiding the main pull of the current. They passed tugs and patrol boats but were not challenged. The traffic thinned and all but disappeared. He dreaded facing the Edwards family more than he had Sam Jacks with the pike pole. He thought of trying to explain. They'd never believe him. He'd said the meanest, most hurting things he could think

220

of. He was through here. He wouldn't blame them if they didn't let him stay the night.

It was early afternoon when he spotted the pilings and turned in. He was surprised and pleased to see the logs they'd gathered were still there. He made *Methuselah* fast beside the old rowboat the three prisoners had come in. He stood on the deck and looked at the buildings across the water that had once been the pasture. The tops of the fence posts showed. The water had gone down some. He looked at the old barn, the house, and the laying house. He remembered the day he'd come here a long time ago—a little over four months ago. That first night Doris Edwards had said, "You'll like it if you become interested, if you let yourself become involved in the activities here."

He thought of Beauty, and how he'd worked with the doctor that night. In this pasture she had run and played in the winter sunshine. He remembered her death with an ache that had never left. He thought of the night in the pasture when Nipper and he had fought off the cougar. He lived over the killing of the cougar. He thought of the days hunting logs on the river, raising the baby chicks. He was even going to miss Junior. He'd become even more involved the past two days. He'd given up everything for the three people who lived in that old house. Things sure work out crazy sometimes, he thought. He picked up the rifle, said, "Come on, Nipper," and dropped into the rowboat.

He rowed across the pasture, past the barn and the laying house, and beached the boat at the foot of the hill. With Nipper beside him he walked up the hill, and climbed the steps to the porch. He stopped, confused. He didn't know how to go in or what to say.

The kitchen door burst open and Jennie rushed at him, blonde hair flying. "Danny! Danny!" She had both arms around him. "You're back! You're back!" She dragged him into the kitchen shouting, "Mom, Pop! Danny's back. He's back!"

He was surrounded. Everyone was talking and laughing at once. Nipper began to bark.

Doris Edwards hugged and kissed him. She was crying.

Mr. Edwards had an arm around his shoulders and squeezed him until his muscles felt numb. "Lord, we're glad you're back!" he said.

Dan was dumbfounded. He said, "That talk the other morning. I didn't mean any of those things."

That stopped them. They looked at him as if they couldn't believe what he'd said. "Why, son, we know that," Mr. Edwards said. "Doris and I played along to help you out."

"You knew all along?"

"When you work partners as long as we have you ought to know something about a man."

"I didn't," Dan said, and felt he'd let Mr. Edwards down.

"I knew from the first, too," Jennie piped up. And when Dan glanced at her, "Well, almost from the first."

"I didn't like what you were doing," Mr. Edwards said. "But you had the bull by the horns and I didn't know what else to do but go along. I figured you had some sort of plan since you knew one of them."

Dan shook his head, "I just hoped something would happen."

Mr. Edwards took the rifle from him and shoved him down in a chair. "We want to know all about it."

"I bet Danny captured those three men and took 'em right in to the police," Jennie said, her brown eyes big.

"Not quite," Dan smiled. He told them what had happened.

"I wanted to phone the police that first morning," Mr. Edwards said. "But it was ten miles to the nearest phone and ten miles back. I was afraid to leave here for that long. I didn't know what might happen next. I let you down, Dan."

"Oh, no." Dan was shocked. "I knew it had to be like that. It worked out fine."

"No thanks to us. But the main thing is you're back and safe."

"When did you eat last?" Doris Edwards asked suddenly.

"About midnight."

She and Jennie were at the refrigerator almost before Dan had finished speaking. They piled food before him. "Nipper hasn't had anything either," Dan said.

They talked calmly now while he and Nipper ate. "How did our logs come through?" Mr. Edwards asked. "I haven't been able to get down there."

"We didn't lose a one."

"Then we've got the new barn," Mr. Edwards said happily. "You know, except for losing the brooder house and the pullets, this flood won't hurt us so badly. In fact, it'll add about an inch of silt topsoil to the land and make it richer than ever."

Dan stopped eating. He put both hands over his eyes and

rested his elbows on the table. He felt shaky and half sick and utterly exhausted. Three days of worry, tension, and lack of sleep had caught up with him.

Doris Edwards said, "Go upstairs to bed, Dan. I'll bet you haven't had a night's sleep since you left."

Dan shook his head and murmured, "What time do we milk?"

"I'll take care of it," Mr. Edwards said.

"You need sleep," Doris Edwards insisted.

"I want to milk." He wanted to see ugly old Junior and Blossom and Ginger and all the rest. Somehow that would make the homecoming complete.

Mr. Edwards nodded. "I'll wake you."

Dan started up the stairs, then stopped and looked back at the three people in the kitchen. He wanted to say something about how glad he was to be back but all he could think of was, "The rifle's still loaded."

"I'll unload the rifle," Mr. Edwards smiled.

Dan had thought he'd never see this room again. But it was just as he'd left it. The piece of pencil he'd wanted so desperately to write the note with still lay on the dresser.

He undressed and stood a moment on the cougar hide, thinking. He felt the softness of the fur under his feet. It was too bad Hank Simmons had to make a trip out here for nothing. But he guessed Hank wouldn't mind. He crawled into bed and pulled the covers over him. The bed was soft and yielding. He stretched luxuriously and closed his eyes. He slept and he was smiling.